I0588124

welcome!
browse, sit awhile or borrow.
but, please
RETURN TO:

Also From the Author

- A LAD FROM SARDINIA **The Adventures of Morgan Harmony**

A High Seas Adventure in The Mediterranean Sea In the 1600's. Story set in prose poetry.

- POETPOURRI **A Labyrinth of Wandering Thought**

A Collection of Short Stories Poetry and Prose Poetry From the Ridiculous to the Sublime.

- A RANGER'S TALE **Jacks' Vendetta**

An Old West adventure revolving around the fledgling band of Texas Rangers in pursuit of the Jacks' gang.

Cowboy Justice series

- COWBOY JUSTICE **On The Border**

A fictional account of an Arizona lawman who joins a vigilante group to rid the influx of illicit drugs and entry by undocumented migrants along the southern U.S. border.

- A CRY FOR JUSTICE **continuing the fight against corruption**

Trafficking and drug-running are ugly, ongoing problems, not just in Arizona, but in every state--and now, as a couple, Frank and his bride feel a shared obligation to follow the desperate cry for help whenever and wherever it presents.

Gumshoe & Fox series

- THE REUNION **a Case of Revocable Trust**

Gumshoe & Fox Mystery

a story that begins with a high school reunion filled with fond memories, a few drinks, some dancing and some back-slapping . . . and ends with murder--not one but four murders. And that's just the start.

The Derelict

A GUMSHOE & FOX CRIME STORY

By

Myron Ferdig

Published by Ferdigwerks
P.O. Box 176
Tujunga, CA 91043
www.ferdigwerks.com

Printed in the United States of America

Prologue

Thick, dank darkness, complete with pungent, foul odors of rotten fish and mold met her as she came back to life. Hands and feet were tightly secured with some kind of cord, leaving her hog-tied on a wooden floor. Three or four minutes of struggling proved useless.

Think, Liz! Think! What happened?

Her last memory was opening her motel door to a set of hairy knuckles smashing into her jaw. Then stars. But before that? . . . She had emailed Gumshoe and faxed some pictures of the people she supposed held the young Maggorie boy against his will . . . oh! and she had taken pictures of them as they boarded a fishing boat called *The Blue Moon.*

As she lay there she could hear *and feel* the ebb and flow of the sea beneath her, coming through the floor; she surmised she was probably now aboard that old, derelict hulk.

This book
is a work of fiction.

The Derelict

A GUMSHOE & FOX
CRIME STORY

Myron Ferdig

1

Sunday, Sept. 29. 2 p.m.
The Crew

"I can already taste the money!" Willie laughed. "In a couple of days we just move in and scoop up the kid and his black book!"

"That's what the boss says. Might not be that easy though," Danny cautioned. "He may have already unloaded the damn thing."

"Or it never left his dad's office," Candy chimed in. "Why would a dude steal his dad's address book? I don't get it. What's the big deal, anyway?"

"Oh, he took it," Willie said with conviction. "And he's still got it. Bet on it. According to the boss it's still listed as available on the dark web. And if he wants that book and the kid, it's a big deal."

The three--Danny Grayling, Willie Burch and Candy Mattis were enjoying a burger and fries at an I-95 frontage road burger joint, just north of Vero Beach, Florida. It was September 29. They had been on the kid's trail since September 26th . . . four days. This would be their biggest score.

Exciting business, this . . . working for their new boss. A fortuitous meeting in a bar outside Camp Lejeune. He asked if they wanted to make some easy money, and ended up promising them $10,000.00 to follow this "Paul" kid, make sure he ended up in Key West, Florida by October 1, even--he had smiled as he said it--even if they had to kidnap Paul.

The boss was even going to pay all their expenses: gas, motel, food and drink. Just keep all the receipts, he said. He would double that fee to $20,000.00 if, without attracting the attention of local authorities, they brought Paul with a certain black binder to an old fishing trawler named *The Blue Moon* in Key West by October 1.

Willie had frowned and more or less demanded an "up-front" $1,000.00 as an expense package, the excess to be returned, or to become part of their overall agreement.

They laughed nervously over their burgers . . . but the boss had smiled at the demand and said, "Young man, you have *cojones*. Maybe we can continue to work together when this job is done." Then he spread ten crisp $100.00 bills on the table in front of them.

With that, their new employer gave Willie a GPS tracking device. "Paul's car is bugged. You can locate him and track him down anytime. Stay close."

They were staying close. Hopefully, they'll be able to befriend him either later today or tomorrow and convince him their boss in Key West is anxious to buy his notebook. If that wouldn't work, they would have to kidnap him.

"Either way," Danny laughed as he dipped a french fry into a small cup of ketchup, "it'll be a good payday."

2

Wednesday, October 2. 4 p.m.
Gumshoe

The flight from LAX to Miami was pleasant enough and from there it was only a short hop to the small Key West airport next to the Naval Air Station. Picking up a reserved Ford Mustang and a map from Alamo I negotiated my way to *The Chelsea House*. It was 4 p.m. Wednesday, October 2.

"Welcome! How may I help you?" came the voice from behind the counter. Teen, fifteen-sixteen I guessed, white shorts, green and white striped tank top. Didn't bother getting up from her leather armchair, but smiled broadly up at me.

"Hello, young lady. I'm Alan Garrett from Los Angeles. I'm looking for my assistant, Liz McConnell. She checked in here a few days ago. I haven't heard from her for a couple of days and I'm a bit concerned."

"Ahh, you must be that private eye fellow! My name is Jennifer," she said, standing, stretching out her hand. She was taller than I thought--maybe 5'6". "Folks call me Squeaky--I guess because I used to laugh funny. Your friend calls herself Fox, right?"

"Yes, I'm that private eye fellow, and yes, Liz calls herself Fox," I said, trying to keep pace with her, "but I wonder about that 'Squeaky' nickname. Sounds like a preteen name which I suspect you've outgrown."

"Oh! Thank you, kind sir! Yes, as a matter of fact, my preteens ended nine years ago. But I think you have a nickname, too. What is it she calls you, Mr. Garrett?" Jennifer searched through her client files and pulled out Room 23, with Liz's business card clipped to it. Giggling, she handed me the card.

"*Gumshoe and Fox.* That's it! *Gumshoe!* Talk about a nickname! Come to think of it, Gumshoe, I haven't seen Fox for a day or two. We sent some faxes to you yesterday or the day before and I haven't seen her since. She's paid up through tomorrow night."

"If you don't mind," I said, "let's grab a key and take a look in her room."

"Sure. Give me a second. I'll call my brother to watch the desk for a couple of minutes."

Little brother was almost as tall as me and weighed as much as the left guard for the Miami Dolphins.

"Two bucks a minute," he frowned to his sister as he walked through the private door behind Jennifer and into the office. "I'm in the middle of a game!" he said emphatically, slamming the door.

"Munch, meet Gumshoe. Gumshoe, my brother Munch. Gumshoe is here looking for his sidekick, Fox, the detective from Room 23."

"That's nice," Munch tapped his watch. "Two bucks a minute," he repeated. Turning to me he added, "Hello, Gumshoe."

On the way to Room 23 Jennifer explained. "Munch plays on-line poker, and when he's hot he hates to be disturbed. Obviously, he's doing well."

"He's not old enough to get involved in that on-line crap is he? How old is he?"

As she unlocked the door, she laughed and turned to me, "Munch--uh, Marvin--is seventeen, a senior this year."

"Let me guess, got his name from eating everything in sight," I smiled.

"My, you are a private detective, aren't you?"

I nodded and touched the front edge of my fedora. We entered.

The room had been ransacked: open, empty suitcase on the bed, clothes strewn over the floor, closet empty, dresser drawers hanging empty. No laptop, purse, wallet or phone. Most disturbing were the few drops of blood on the floor just inside the door.

Jennifer kept repeating, "Oh, No!" over and over, but I breathed a sigh of relief . . . Fox was not to be seen. Why had she not used her phone or laptop to communicate with me? Hopefully, she was somewhere safe. But the blood, even though it was minimal, was unsettling.

"I'll stay here, Jennifer. Leave the room as it is. I'll straighten it up. But you can hustle back to the office to minimize your losses. Two bucks a minute adds up. Oh," I added, "would you call the police to have a forensics team here to check this room for prints?"

Jennifer took one last look around, shaking her head. "Oh! Of course," she replied and left me to assess the distressed room.

I didn't have long to wait--just minutes later a two-man detail from the Key West Police pulled up. After introductions and a few questions, they went through the unit, found four sets of prints--one of them belonging to Liz from the number of them--the others scattered here and there throughout the room.

The prints identified a couple of names: Willie Burch and Candy Mattis, two small-time low-lifes from New York. They were a long way from home ... but then, so was I. It was a start. I now had names to go with my pictures. The room's phone rang. It was Jennifer. "Police Chief wants to see you within the hour."

3

Thursday, October 3. 5:20 p.m.
Hector

The chief, Hector Rodriguez--sometimes just plain Chief to his fellow officers, was waiting for me with a torrent of questions, starting with, "Who are you?"

"Hi. Alan Garrett, Sir. Private investigator from Manhattan Beach, California. I'm here to locate my associate, Liz McConnell who has been here on assignment."

"Where in hell is Manhattan Beach, California? And what was her assignment to bring her, and now you, to this side of our country?"

"A private matter involving the son of an Air Force General, Sir."

"How do you know this general, Garrett, and what's his name, and in addition, why did you take the assignment?"

"I know both general and his son, Sir. Until I retired I served under the general as an AFOSI officer. His son went missing. He wanted it pursued under the radar."

"The general's name?"

"I'd rather not say, Sir. He doesn't want the government or military involved."

"What's the AFOSI?" Rodriguez continued.

"The Air Force Office of Special Investigations. An enforcement arm of the Air Force, seeking out and bringing to justice corruption within."

"Alright, Garrett. Don't do anything rash. Keep me in the loop. I'll do the same. By the way, what was your associate's last position?"

"A cafe near the water. She sent pictures of an old trawler, *The Blue Moon.* She thought the son might be held there."

"Then we may have a serious problem, Garrett. *The Blue Moon* was cut from her mooring around midnight just last night. She was dragged out about two miles and burned to the waterline. By the time the Coast Guard arrived she had gone under. They had a team of divers out there all morning. No report in as yet."

I felt a sudden, momentary rush of panic grip my gut. Immediately I thought, *Oh, Liz, where are you, you silly goose?* Next, my mind's Rolodex spun through a rash of morbid tragedies; but within milliseconds Alan Garrett returned.

"Chief, would you point me toward that cafe near the water?"

4

Tuesday, October 1. 11: 50 p.m.
Fox

Thick, dank darkness, complete with pungent, foul odors of rotten fish and mold met her as she came back to life. Hands and feet were tightly secured with some kind of cord, leaving her in a fetal position on a wooden floor. Three or four minutes of struggling proved useless.

Think, Liz! Think! What happened?

Her last memory was opening her motel door to a set of hairy knuckles smashing into her jaw. Then stars. But before that? . . . She had emailed Gumshoe and faxed some pictures of the people she supposed held the young Maggorie boy against his will . . . oh! and she had taken pictures of them as they boarded a fishing boat called *The Blue Moon.*

As she lay there she could hear *and feel* the ebb and flow of the sea beneath her, coming through the floor; she surmised she was probably now aboard *The Blue Moon.*

How long had she been here? She didn't know, but the nausea was overwhelming . . . she heaved out the rest of the whatever had been in her stomach then struggled to a sitting position and took a physical inventory. Her head felt like a pumpkin with all of its seeds scrambled after a carving knife had turned it into a garish, orange Jack-o-Lantern.

Her tongue felt its way along the upper row, then the lowers . . . all accounted for . . . but pain shot through her lower right jaw accompanied by the taste of blood. Gingerly she explored that area further; the inside of the cheek felt like spaghetti.

Another thing she remembered: Gumshoe had warned her to avoid risks, but Liz McConnell (Fox) was well within her field of expertise . . . or so she thought . . . but the abductors had seen her! Unfortunate! *You should have listened to Gumshoe! You blew it bad, Fox!*

"Anybody here?" She started with a whisper, then increased her volume to a normal speaking voice. "Paul, are you in this hole with me? Can you hear me? Can anyone hear me?" But the only sounds she heard were those of water against the sides of the craft where she was being held.

Her enclosure was small; she could sense the closeness of the walls. She tried to pierce the darkness for any shapes, but couldn't manage a shadow. She sat for a few moments and formulated a plan. Dropping back to her side, Fox began to roll until she banged into a wall.

The floor was surprisingly free of the imagined slime and debris she was afraid she would encounter. She breathed a sigh of relief. "That was easy . . . now I need to get rid of these ropes and get out of here."

Just hearing herself speak was comforting. The silence had been unnerving. She sat up, put her back to the wall as much as she could manage, and concentrated on her bindings.

Fifteen minutes later her wrists were chafed and terribly painful, but she now had some "wiggle" room. For the first time since her head exploded Fox felt a burst of energy and hope. She continued her task.

She heard the sound at first: the unmistakable splutter of a marine diesel engine. Then she felt her confined space undulating with motion. The engine noise continued to grow stronger, then abruptly a definite change . . . possibly a shift to neutral. Then a full stop.

After a moment of silence came the scuffling of boots on the deck above, mixed with muffled, gruff voices. Fox held her breath, listening intently. Something major was happening. She pulled harder on her cords. She could almost slip a wrist free.

The floor and walls suddenly shuddered and lurched, throwing Fox forward; the diesel revved, the vessel was moving! "Gumshoe!" she whispered, "I'm in real trouble."

5

Wednesday, October 2. 5:45 p.m.
Gumshoe

The Hungry Pelican Cafe was easy to find. On North Roosevelt Avenue overlooking a few fishing charters. Until yesterday, according to Marge, a young, energetic waitress, you could see the old *Blue Moon* almost directly across from them.

"It's a shame, you know?" she said. "That old trawler was almost 100 years old. She was a familiar landmark around here. Some of the old boys, like Ernie and Sam over there in the corner, come in here for coffee every day and spin stories for the tourists. They still have stories to tell, but now," . . . Marge's voice trailed off in genuine remorse . . . "now she's gone. The gall of some people, you know?"

"Was she seaworthy at all, Marge?" I asked.

"I don't think so. Sorry. I got customers. Go ask the boys." She jerked a thumb toward the corner booth and picked up a fresh coffee carafe from the Krups machine. I walked over to talk to the boys.

"Mind if I sit down, fellas?"

"No, but you don't look like a fisherman or a tourist. Are you Coast Guard? Did you find her?" the one named Ernie asked.

"No. I'm looking for my assistant, Fox. I'm here from California. Last I talked with her she was in a cafe around here somewhere."

"That would be here," the other one said, holding out his calloused, weathered hand. As I took it, "Sam," he said. "We're waiting for the Coast Guard to confirm she's actually gone."

"Alan," I responded. "No word yet?"

"No. Still waiting. You waiting, too?"

"Yes. I'm worried Fox may have been on *The Blue Moon*. Here's her picture." I showed them a photo of Liz.

The two men looked at each other and then at me. "Yeah. She's been here a couple of times. Why would she be on *The Blue Moon?*" Ernie asked.

Ignoring his question, I pulled from my pocket the pictures Liz had faxed to me and laid them on the table. "Have you seen these fellows?"

"Sure have. Day before yesterday. Came in with another young fella, no more than a teen. Sat right there," Sam pointed at a table in the center of the dining room.

"Yeah, waiting for a fifth one . . . the one they called *the Boss*. While waiting, they all had a piece of pie. But their boss didn't show up. We saw someone waving from across the road, we figured it was *the Boss*.

"That's right," Ernie agreed, "so these fellas walked out together. Last we saw, they crossed the road, shook hands with that other fella and headed out in the direction of our old gal . . . but your lady friend wasn't with them. Did they sink our boat?"

Marge came around with coffee. We held our cups out for refills.

"I don't know," I said. "I think so. Sorry about your boat, but right now I'm worried about my lady friend and that young fellow. These three," I said, pointing at the photos, "are definitely bad ones. I suspect *the Boss* is responsible for sinking your boat."

The front door opened. Three white uniformed men walked in. We were about to receive the latest news concerning *The Blue Moon*.

6

Wednesday, October 2. Late Afternoon
Coast Guard

Chairs scraped as the three seated themselves at a table next to us. They tipped their coffee mugs upright and nodded to Marge. One said to her, "Bring us some cherry pie, too, Marge. Been a tough day."

Another of them turned to my companions: "Ernie, Sam. It's that old derelict, *The Blue Moon* alright. She's gone for good, just as we figured. Damn shame."

A tear almost made it down Ernie's cheek, but he brushed it aside. "Yeah. Well, Bill, I guess we all have to go sometime. At least she died at sea. Better than rotting away next to a shopping mall."

Sam grunted in agreement, and everyone in the place who heard nodded their heads at the simple eloquence voiced by Ernie.

"Bill, my name is Alan Garrett. I'm a private detective working on a case. I've be…"

"Sir!" one of the other Guardsmen sat up straight and interrupted. "We just spoke with Hector; he told us you were in town all the way from Manhattan Beach. A former AFOSI agent, right? We were going to look you up. I'm Henry. Commander Henry Waite. This is Fernando, Sir. We have some things to discuss; rather do it in private, Sir."

"Now?" I asked, somewhat puzzled, but fearing the worst.

"No, but tomorrow morning, let's say 0:700?" Fernando joined in. "You have some pictures we would like to look at, perhaps have copies made for us."

"Certainly," I agreed. "In the meantime, I'll send copies to your phone. The police chief asked to be kept in the loop; happy to meet you there. Then everyone will be equally informed."

Sam and Ernie looked at me with renewed interest. "Cop?" Sam asked.

"Naw," Ernie supplied . . . "used to be an M.P. Must still have some clout in Washington . . . am I right, Alan?"

"Close, but no cigar, fellas." I laughed, throwing my hands in the air. "I'm a simple private eye, looking for my associate, who just happened to disappear while on assignment here in Florida."

"Bullshit! . . . uh, respectfully, of course," Sam snorted. The tables next to us burst out with laughter.

Bill leaned over and said, "Ernie, this fellow spent twenty years as the military equivalent of a division leader in the FBI; like an Admiral or Commander of the 8th Fleet, maybe even like General Eisenhower in the Second World War."

As my two table mates were looking at me with

renewed respect I shook my head and said my own, "Bullshit. All lies fellas," I laughed. Sam only grunted.

I got up to leave. Everyone stood. Sam and Ernie smiled, said their goodbyes, Marge yelled from across the room, "Come back. Best coffee in town."

* * *

I swung by a local liquor store and picked up a bottle of Martell . . . then five minutes later I walked into the motel office. Jennifer wasn't there, replaced by an older, no-nonsense gent. I added my name to Room 23 and added one more night.

"That's the lady that's gone missing?" When I nodded, he added, "Hopefully, she'll turn up tomorrow. Have a pleasant evening."

I entered Room 23, expecting to find it in chaos, but someone had beat me to the clean-up. All of Liz's belonging had been restored to drawers and closets; only my belongings were still undisturbed in my closed suitcase on the newly-made bed.

A note on the dresser said *"Liz, I pray you're back and safe. Alan, I know all about you, from Liz. She says--and I believe--you're a great boss. Stay safe."* It was signed simply N. W.

They say a reasonable tip for a housekeeper is two or three bucks a night but this went well beyond any expectations. I wrote my own note to N.W. and left it along with a twenty dollar bill. Then I added a smiley face note, *"Don't expect this amount the rest of my stay."*

I flipped the TV on. Then poured myself a couple of fingers of Martell. It was 8:55 p.m. here, but back home it was three hours earlier. I called Pop. (Yes, Pop is my dad, a retired firefighter. He and mom had turned the family home over to me many years ago. Mom is no longer with us; Pop was going to move out, but at my insistence he now lives upstairs, and we share many of the household duties. He has a lady friend, a Mrs. Rita Mason . . . which may or may not develop into something more than a casual friendship. Time will tell...)

So as I said, I called Pop.

"Have you found her, Son?"

"Not yet, Pop. But I'm hopeful. How is the Gunn and Gunn debacle coming along?"

"We're making some progress, but it's a marathon job."

We spent a few minutes discussing that previous case and its subsequent fallout, then after some small talk about Manhattan Beach weather, fishing on the pier, my Cadillac, we discussed any calls or messages of which I should be made aware.

"Your friend, Rachel, is lonely, Son. Wants to know when you're coming back." Pop laughed. I used *Bullshit* for the second time today, then we hung up. I poured another two fingers of Martell, sat on the bed and watched the muted screen on channel 4.

The volume in my head needed no competition from the tube. My mind was whirring with various thoughts--where is Fox? And for that matter, young Paul Maggorie? Who dragged *The Blue Moon* out two miles and torched her? And why? What do the Coast Guard boys wish to discuss?

I picked up the remote, turned up the volume on the TV. CBS was talking about the upcoming October Democratic debate. Damn! We just finished the September blah,blah,blah and here it comes again. *We're going to lose this country to idiots!*

The room became suddenly small, cramped, stuffy. I turned the TV off, dropped a couple of ice cubes in my glass, topped it off with Martell and walked outside. The temperature was a bit cooler than when I flew in at 4 p.m. I could even feel a slight breeze.

A marina wasn't far. I started across Roosevelt Avenue, heading for the bobbing mainsails still visible in the darkening sky. A female voice behind stopped me.

"Gumshoe!"

The only one that knows me by that name down here is Fox, I thought, and wheeled. But it wasn't Fox who came running across the highway.

"Nice night for a walk. May I join you?"

"Why, of course you may, Jennifer." (Oh! I'd forgotten about Jennifer.) "Just thought I'd stretch my legs; been sitting in a plane, then in the Chief's office and the cafe. I usually run a few miles every day. I may have to curtail that as a regimen while I'm here. The humidity may be too much for an old man."

"I'll run with you, but it must be early . . . 6:30 a.m. or so. Too hot after that, and my first class is at 8:20 a.m."

"There's a college here in Key West?"

"Florida Keys Community College, majoring in Fishing and Fisheries, but I may switch or add Police Action or Criminology. I'm in no hurry to move up to Miami to go for a Bachelor's."

"Either one sounds good, Jennifer. You have some fine practical teachers--Fisheries, police and a Coast Guard detachment here. You could knock on some doors, apply for a practicum . . . remember the squeaky wheel principle."

"Cute play on words, Gumshoe."

We were now on the approach to the front of the main wharf going into the marina. A yacht was negotiating one of the outer slips; her spotlights guided on her final approach. By the time we neared, sailors were casting their lines to others waiting on the dock to tie her off. Then the yacht emptied, it's nine or ten occupants approached us. They were speaking in a dialect or language I didn't quite recognize. As we closed the distance, we exchanged niceties in perfect English with the three Caucasian gents in front. One was obviously the leader--about my age--the others younger. Those in the rear were darker-skinned, probably hired sailors. Without stopping for tea, we sized each other up, then carried on and passed each other.

Something was wrong with that picture. I chose for the moment to keep my thoughts from Jennifer, but as we walked to the end of the pier and started back, Jennifer mentioned the yacht.

"She came in late. It's now after 11 p.m."

"I agree," I said. "Isn't there a harbor master?"

"There is. Buck Watters during the day, and Kate Moore takes over at 5 p.m. Works until 11 p.m."

"Perhaps the vessel has a cruising license, which gives them an exemption to a face to face meeting," I suggested.

"Wow, Gumshoe! They can do that? I thought you were an Air Force investigator. I have a lot to learn and I've been here all my life."

"Jot down the name and call letters of that yacht... I'll check it out in the morning. Anything else you noticed, Jennifer?"

"No, Sir."

"What language were they speaking?"

"English. At least some were."

"And the others?"

"Oh! I don't know, Gumshoe. I wasn't really paying attention."

"A bit like Spanish, but not quite. Portuguese maybe?"

"Oh! And they were flying the Brazilian flag," she added.

We walked back across the road to the motel. My mind was wrestling with the sailors we had just encountered. Did I recognize any of them? No, but they reeked of *evil*. It was written on their faces, especially the three walking in the lead.

"Jennifer, can we make it 6 a.m.?" I asked. "I have a meeting with the Coast Guard at 7."

"6 a.m. is fine. I'll see you in front of the office," Jennifer agreed.

I bid her a good night. It was after 11 p.m.

7

Thursday, October 3.
Early morning run

6 a.m. comes much earlier in Florida for a California boy than 6 a.m. in Manhattan Beach.

After parting from Jennifer, I emptied my suitcase into the bottom drawers of the dresser in my room, poured another short Martell, sipped it while watching the tail end of the 11 o'clock news, hit the shower and finally hit the sheets . . . all the while worrying about Fox and wondering about that group from the yacht. When 6 a.m. came I was standing in front of the motel office, not having slept a wink. As I said, 6 a.m. comes much earlier in Florida.

"You're right on time, Gumshoe," Jennifer laughed. "Sleep well?"

"I'd be lying if I said yes," I answered. "Better question, did I sleep? No fault of the room or the bed; just too many things going through the brain, raising their hands and demanding time."

"Cute. So where to?" she asked.

"You know the area, young lady. How about up through town a couple of miles, then cut left to the water and come back along the beach?"

"Sounds great! I've never run through town before. Usually down the beach and back up."

"Fine if that suits you, let's do th..."

"No!" Jennifer laughed, "who knows . . . could create enough interest among early risers to start a running group."

Jennifer proved to be a good running mate; for almost the entire first leg of our run she kept up stride for stride. Then, as we were approaching an intersection, I saw her checking her watch. "We've traveled a mile and three quarters. It's 6:17– time to hang a left."

"Let's do it," I agreed. "You doing okay?"

"Sure. The beach is, I think, six blocks. Feel like a sprint?" Jennifer challenged.

"No cramps yet. You're on! Go!"

She was twenty feet in front of me before I took my first steps. Fortunately both the early morning auto and foot traffic was sparse. We covered the distance without a car in sight. Her toes hit the water first. The girl could sprint!

After a minute with hands on knees to catch our breath, we started the journey back. A group of surfers in wet suits was out in a pack 100 yards out or so in the water, waiting for the next surge of the morning tide. The Keys are not known for surfing, but they'll take what they get, I suppose. We smiled and waved.

"Have you ever surfed?" I asked Jennifer as we jogged along.

"Not really. Boogie board is all . . . so far," she waggled one finger at me and laughed. "Someday. And you?"

"I live right above the Manhattan Beach Pier in California. Surfed almost from the time I could walk," I answered, "but I haven't surfed in years."

Jennifer glanced at her watch. "We have less than a mile to go. Should be in good shape, time-wise. A couple of minutes to cool down in your room and the quick trip to your meeting," she assured me.

She looked up the beach. "Uh, oh! what's this?" She said it the same time I thought it.

"Not sure," I frowned. Not far up the beach and out on the sand a police cruiser was just leaving. A group of black-suited surfers along with a few sunbathers was gathered around at the water's edge; we joined them.

"What's up, people?" I asked one of the surfers.

"We just pulled a drowning lady out of the water, that's what's up, mister. She was damn near dead when we found her. Must have been almost a half mile out there, bobbing on a board in the water.

We thought it was some debris from a recent launch at the Cape, so Jones, there, paddled out to retrieve it. He threw her on his board and paddled in to the rest of us; surprised the hell out of us."

Question after question popped to the surface, but I could only come up with, "Is she okay?" I called for the guy named Jones, "Hey, Jones! Is she going to be okay?"

Jones was at my shoulder. He chimed in, "She was still breathing. Her face and arms were pretty battered, bruised and badly sunburned. She'd swallowed a lot of sea water, but between us and the ambulance fellas we pumped that out of her."

"Where did the ambulance take her?" I asked.

"Probably Advanced Urgent Care," Jennifer cut in. "I know where they are. It's close, Gumshoe." She was already tugging on my arm and heading further south. "We can be there just as fast as we can run to the motel. It's in the same direction."

We were ushered into a waiting room along with a lone policeman, Officer Gary Thune. The time was 6:50 a.m. I surprised the officer when I called a number and asked for Chief Rodriguez.

"Chief, Alan Garrett here. I'm going to be a bit late. I'm at the hospital. A lady was pulled out of . . . Oh! You heard? Of course you heard. Yes, I haven't seen her yet but I believe she's my missing associate, Liz. Yes, Sir. Thank you, Sir. Yes, I'll call." "So, you think you know the lady?" Officer Thune asked. "Then you can identify her, right? Good. I should be able to get out of here early."

8

Thursday, October 3. 6:50 a.m.
The odor of evil

Her face and arms were wrapped in white gauze, as was, I suspected, the rest of her body. Only her eyes were visible, and they were open for only a few milliseconds. Otherwise, closed. She was heavily sedated but she was definitely my associate, Liz McConnell—better known as Fox.

Thune tipped his hat. "I'm out of here if you're sure this is your lady. And you are sure, right?"

"Yes. I don't need to unwrap her. I saw those eyes."

Jennifer and I spoke with the nurse in charge to know the state of Liz's burns.

"She's a very fortunate young lady," the nurse shook her head. "The sea is very unforgiving, but your friend will survive. She has second degree burns over much of her body, but let me assure you, treatment today is better than even five years ago. Give me your contact number. No sense in hanging around. I'll call you when you may visit. My name is Jackie, by the way."

"Thank you, Jackie. I'm staying at the *Chelsea House*, where Jennifer works."

"Which my family owns," Jennifer corrected me. "Lived there all my life."

"I know that place; almost right around the corner from us," Jackie exclaimed. "Okay neighbors, I'll call."

We jogged back to the motel. I thanked Jennifer for the morning workout, told her to add five more days to my stay and walked to my room.

I spent five minutes in the shower, then into fresh outfit and drove to police headquarters for the meeting with the chief and the three Coast Guard fellas.

A desk sergeant showed me into the police conference room. The chief sitting at the center of a table that could easily sit ten. He was flanked by three of his detectives. The three members of the Coast Guard were ranged around the table leaving a space for me between them. After the formal introductions--complete with handshakes, the chief asked, "Is the lady in the hospital your associate, Mr. Garrett?"

"Yes, Sir. We weren't able to speak with her; she's in tough shape but the nurse says she'll pull through."

"Would it trouble you to finish filling out this report for me, Garrett?" Hector passed a clipboard in my direction. "Officer Thune started it, but he doesn't know your associate's movements prior to ending up in the water."

I frowned. *A bit unusual*, I thought . . . but, what the heck. I took the form from him and jotted down her full name, address and place of employment, the when and why Liz was here, how she had happened to take some pictures of some unsavory characters , how she called me when she suspected she had been noticed, and how she had subsequently disappeared, all of which prompted my flying in. I passed it back to the chief. He set it down without looking at it.

One of Hector's underlings, Mike Broderick, picked up the clipboard and read through it, then looking at me, questioned my legal standing in Florida. "Are you licensed to operate here, Garrett? We frown upon wild west tactics here on this side of the river."

"I can assure you, Mike, I have complied with every protocol the state demands, right down to carry permits for my associate and me. Insofar as licensing, my company is registered with every state on the Atlantic seaboard, including Florida."

"We'd like to see the paperwork and permits." That came from another of Hector's lieutenants, one Rubin Benites.

The representatives from the Coast Guard had remained silent until now. Henry spoke first.

"Listen up, fellas. We met with Mr. Garrett yesterday. He wanted a meeting; we suggested a get-together today, he insisted that we keep you all in the loop. That's the only reason we've joined you here at police headquarters. Otherwise we'd be meeting at our office. The three of us can vouch for Garrett's stellar reputation as an investigator and for his integrity. Stop the pettiness; we have things to discuss."

Fernando took over. "*The Blue Moon* went down two miles off our coast the night of October one. We know she was a derelict craft, tied to her moorings for decades, so she was obviously towed to sea by a motor vessel and scuttled–burned to the waterline before she went down. The obvious question, why?"

"And who?" Hector added. "Before she disappeared, Garrett's associate took photos of three punks in the *Hungry Pelican*. I think we've all seen these photos by now," he said, tossing copies of the photos on the table.

"And then," I joined in, "according to Sam and Ernie at the cafe, we have an older fellow and a kid joining them. They sat for a few minutes, had a piece of pie, then headed across the road toward *The Blue Moon*. The older fellow was identified simply as the *Boss*."

Fernando continued, "Our divers made a couple of discoveries we're sharing here for the first time: three bodies were found in the engine room—two males, one female— all in their twenties, all shot in the head. In the compartment we'll call the fish hold they found evidence of a captive female whose wrists and ankles were only recently freed from being tightly bound by small diameter ropes. The ropes were saturated with blood from an obviously tortuous ordeal."

"It appears, now," Bill finished the narrative, "which we will soon confirm, she is Alan's assistant, Liz. Thank God she appears to have miraculously escaped before the boat was torched and sunk. Perhaps in the coming days she can provide some important intel to answer that all important question, *why*." No one spoke for several seconds.

I broke the silence. "A yacht came into the marina just across from the *Chelsea House* last night. She tied off after 11 p.m. Flies a Brazilian flag. She's called <u>Bordereau</u>. A cute play on words by the way. I assume she cost a pretty penny.

We, that is Jennifer from the motel and I, met the crew as they came down the gangway. No one met them to check their papers as they hit dry land. Perhaps you folks have a different way of dealing with foreign craft coming into harbor at such an hour. It just seemed rather peculiar to me. I would have thought Coast Guard, Harbor Master, someone," I shrugged. "I have her call letters," I said, pulling a note from my shirt pocket, handing it to Henry.

"That yacht's been accounted for," Bill acknowledged. "She came in September 27. We boarded her at that time. Captain applied for and received a cruising license. In our waters until, what did we approve, Henry, October 11?"

Henry nodded, looking at the time. "That's correct, Sir. Two weeks," he noted, reading from his screen. "All carry Brazilian passports. Captain Bosignion is European . . . Austrian, I think. He speaks perfect English. Total of four officers and a crew of six. No females."

"Did they have a specific itinerary?" I pushed for more information.

"Vacationing. A pleasure cruise. Their schedule includes a round trip to Miami starting, uh, starting tomorrow. Back here on October 10 for refueling and gone the following morning. All subject to an earlier departure, of course."

"Why the interest in that particular yacht, Garrett?" Hector queried. "We have pleasure boats, yachts and fishing trawlers in and out of our marinas all day, every day."

"Just a feeling, Sir. After twenty years of investigating the criminal element, evil has a certain inescapable odor about it. I sensed that evil as Jennifer and I passed that yacht crew last night."

"You can't be serious, Garrett," Mike Broderick said sarcastically, "relying on some mumbo-jumbo feeling to establish the certainty of evil."

Hector continued the theme, "Ooohhhh, do you feel the certainty of evil present in this room, Garrett?" The police chief asked sarcastically hands flailing the air. Some of the others laughed nervously.

"Matter of fact, yes, Sir, I do," I said soberly.

Everyone at the table watched as I reached for the cream in the center of the table, poured an inch in my mug, then filled it with coffee from one of three carafes.

"What is that supposed to mean?" the police chief asked.

I simply shrugged and gulped down my coffee. "Gentlemen," I nodded, set my fedora squarely on my head . . .

"I'm just beginning my investigation. Let's all keep one another in the loop." I set the mug carefully on the table. "I'm on my way to the hospital." I felt seven pairs of eyes staring at my backside as I exited the room.

Did I actually feel an aura of evil as I sat in the midst of those in that room? No, not tangibly, but there was a negative presence; might as well throw it out there, see if anything shakes loose.

9

Thursday, October 3. 8:40 a.m.
The Sterile Room

I'm not a fan of hospitals, I've been in several--each visit generally associated with tragedy. This one I'm praying will have a better outcome.

I gave the front desk Liz' name; the young man gave me a quizzical look and a room number--410.

"Let me call the nurse's station on the fourth floor before you go up. As I told her father and her brother, you may not be able to see her yet. The last thing I was told was she isn't in her assigned room yet; she's still in the Sterile Room."

"When were they here?" My spine began to freeze; the hair on my arms stood straight up. "Did they proceed up to the fourth floor?"

"Yes, they did, at uh . . ." he checked his log, "at 7:36 a.m. . . . That's about a half hour ago. What's the problem? Who are you, by the way?"

"Her boss. Call police headquarters. Tell them Garrett needs them here right now. And where's the Sterile Room?"

He gave me directions as he picked up the phone.

I raced to the elevator, up to the top (fourth) floor and found the nurses' station.

"You have a patient, Liz, in the Sterile Room. My name is Alan Garrett. I need to see her now."

The nurse, an older lady with a name badge that said Nell, smiled at me. "We sent her father and brother away already," the nurse informed me. "No one is to be in that room. You may observe her through the window just as they did. Door is right there," she said, pointing across the hallway.

I walked across the hall, and peered through the wired glass observation window. The mummy in the bed was breathing steadily and quietly. *Thank God,* I told myself.

Back to the nurse. "Nell, the lady across the hall is my associate. Those calling themselves relatives are not. I'm having the police come. Anything you remember about those men, please let the police know . . . age, hair color, limp, tattoo, scar, anything."

I continued before she could do more than nod her head, "Can you keep the door under lock and key? I want no one in there except a qualified burn nurse who can be trusted. You have a nurse, Jackie. Is she such a nurse?"

"Jackie? Of course. All of our staff are top-notch."

"I'd like her to be assigned to Liz as a priority. Can you make that happen?"

"You can't come in here and make such demands, Mr. Garrett. We have rules, assignments, priorities. This is a hospital, not a shoe factory. And just why do you want Jackie, specifically?"

"She was the incoming nurse when Liz was admitted, and we felt an immediate affinity. No offense intended, Nell."

"Asked and answered honestly, Mr. Garrett. No offense taken. Now who is *we*, so I can be prepared for a second person making similar demands of me on my floor?"

A sarcastic gaze fixed itself upon my eyes. I felt the urge, and was about to look away, when Officer Thune stepped out of the elevator.

"What's the problem, Garrett?"

"Two people impersonating father and brother of the burn victim from yesterday tried to visit her this morning. I'd like a police presence to watch over her while she's here, and a sketch artist to work with the nurses to get descriptions while it's fresh."

"Sounds reasonable. I'll call the chief. We can probably spare a couple of rookies for a few hours each."

"Thanks, detective," I smiled. "And the artist?"

"Best I can do is get descriptions." He turned to Nell. "Who saw the men, Ma'am?"

In all, Thune interviewed five nurses, three on the fourth floor, two at the front desk. It was noted that the two impostors didn't sign out, nor were they seen leaving the hospital. I stayed outside the Sterile Room until the first shift of officers came to watch the door--young black dude, Timothy White. We chatted for a few minutes, I handed him my card, gave him a quick synopsis of who and why his presence was requested, shook his hand and then, rather than the elevator, I took the stairs.

Up and down both sets—one at either end of the small hospital, and then I walked the corridors of each floor, carefully noting visitors and personnel . . . especially the shoes. (They say that shoes are the most obvious clue that someone doesn't belong.) I saw nothing that raised a flag.

The next hour I spent driving, exploring Key West, all the while thinking about Fox's ordeal and escape, and worrying about young Paul Maggorie. I should call his dad, the general . . . bring him up to date, like, *"Nothing further to report, Sir, but my associate is in the hospital. She reports having seen him just before she was captured. She escaped but the boat she saw Paul walking toward burned and sank and . . ."* Shit! What am I supposed to tell him?

It was time to head back to the *Chelsea House.*

10

Thursday, October 3. 1:10 p.m.
A Date

I pulled into the parking space for Room 23, and before going in I walked to the office. Jennifer was behind the desk.

"Gumshoe! Hello! How are your legs?"

"What?" I asked, a bit confused. "That's a strange question to ask me, young lady. My legs are just fine. How are your legs, Jennifer?"

"I meant after our run. I sat in class for two minutes and my legs started cramping up. I'm not used to running I guess. It's good for me, though. Shall we do it every morning?" She suddenly stood up, and with a painful smile said, "Another one . . . sorry."

"Possibly. Right now I want to pay for a full week." I pulled out my wallet.

"Put your credit card away," Jennifer said, waving off my stretched out hand. "How was your meeting . . . and more importantly, how is Fox? I know you went to see her."

"And how do you know that?" I asked.

"That's who you are, Gumshoe. Anyone in trouble would be grateful to have you on their side."

"And you got all that from a morning run followed by leg cramps?"

"And a psychology class . . . don't forget the psychology class," she laughed. "So, how is she?"

"She's in a special room for the time being, and I guess, she's easily subject to infection. No visitors allowed. But I saw her. She was sedated and asleep." (I wouldn't disclose her father and brother's visit. Just cause ten extra minutes of worry.)

"It will have to be 6:00 a.m. every morning I'm able," I said

"Wha. . . oh! Okay, you're on." Jennifer beamed. "And if you're not able, you'll call me the night before, right?"

"No. I simply won't be there."

"Crap! So much for my psychology class," Jennifer muttered. "Here I thought I was doing so well."

"What'd you expect? '*Sweetie, sorry . . . won't be able to make it in the morning*' . . . never happen, Squeaky," I pushed my fedora further back on my head.

"I was afraid you'd say that, Alan. So much for having a steady date." We laughed. I opened the door to leave. "Hey! Wait a minute. What about your meeting this morning, Gumshoe?"

"Not much to report. Just a group of men sitting around a table, agreeing that a crime had been committed, but no one knows where to go from there. Coffee was okay, though," I said.

"Did you mention the yacht that came in so late?"

"I mentioned the yacht," I confirmed.

"And your thoughts about the characters on the yacht?"

I rolled my eyes. "Yes, Mother, I mentioned them as well. Whatever I brought up was largely debunked by the Coast Guard boys and the police. I guess I'm on my own with my hunches and gut feelings."

"I'm pulling for you, Gumshoe. I've been thinking about the crew that came off the yacht. I think you were right."

"Bullshit, Squeaky. You're just saying that."

"No, it's true. And don't call me Squeaky anymore; I've dropped that nickname. From now on, I'm simply Jennifer."

"I approve, Jennifer or Jen. Now if you'll excuse me, I need to make some phone calls."

"Okay. If you need some help while you're here, and Fox is in the hospital, let me know."

"I'll keep that in mind," I smiled and closed the office door.

11

Thursday, October 3. 4 p.m.
Fox Unwrapped

Jackie took the elevator to the fourth floor. She checked in with Nell, asked about the policeman sitting across the hall and frowned.

"Does Mr. Garrett know?" she asked.

"Oh, yes. He's the one who demanded security for Liz," Nell answered. "He also demanded that you be in charge of her," Nell laughed. "I told him she was in good hands with any of our staff.

There is a problem, though, Jackie. This morning two men tried to get to her by pawning themselves off as her relatives."

Jackie's eyes widened, but she said nothing. She changed into a clean frock and, nodding to officer White, entered the Sterile Room.

She began by putting fresh, wet cotton toweling on arms and face which woke Liz from a fitful sedative-induced sleep.

"Liz," she whispered. "Liz, do you know where you are?" Only a blank look met her. "You're in the hospital in Key West, Dear. Don't try to say anything right now. There will be time. Just listen.

You escaped kidnappers, ended in the ocean, swam or were carried by the tide almost to shore where some surfers brought you in. You have rope burns on your wrists and legs, and sunburn over much of the rest. We're treating you with cool water, aloe vera and other ointments. Your face is quite battered from an apparent beating, and blistered from the sun, so again, don't try to speak . . . perhaps two or three more days."

Jackie unwrapped the towels from Liz' legs . . . not nearly so burned . . . and applied ointment and new towels there as well, speaking reassuringly and calmly as she did so. But then she woke Liz out of her sedation.

"Mr. Alan Garrett is here in Key West. He wants to see you as soon as you are able; so get better."

Liz tried to rise in the bed, but the pain was too severe.

"No, no, no, not yet, dear. I've spoken with him, he knows your condition. Just be patient. He comes to see you, but we can't let him in this room until your open wounds heal a bit more."

Liz tried again to sit. She tried to mouth a word but it didn't make any sense . . . something like *Gus.*   Jackie lifted a tube of cold water to her lips. She swallowed.

"*Puh,*" she whispered.

"You're welcome, Sweetie. I'll be back later."

Jackie smiled and left the room, walked back to the nurse's station. She picked up the phone and called the *Chelsea House.* "Room 23, please."

"Mr. Garrett, Jackie at the hospital. I told you I'd call when you may visit your associate. Not just yet, but she's getting stronger. Come at 7 p.m. I think you may be able to spend a few minutes with her."

12

Thursday, October 3.
Mid-Afternoon
Phone Calls

My first call was to the General. It was time.

"Sir, your son, Paul is apparently in the hands of a criminal element. He was last seen two days ago with three young, small-time crooks out of New York and an unknown older man. The three younger were found dead yesterday, we have no photos of the fourth."

I filled the general in on all the facts as I knew them, leaving nothing out. Maggorie listened intently, then sighed.

"Garrett, this is serious! Everything hinges upon information your associate can give you. I'm afraid the documents that boy took may have already done irreparable damage."

"What was it he took, Sir? And why?"

"Paul is seventeen, Garrett. Becoming a young man, his mother and I decided to increase his privileges, especially since he finished high school just after basketball season was over--that is, January. He was given a prepaid credit card, and we increased his curfew time to midnight.

Then we discovered he had begun using marijuana. We put him on restriction, took away his cell phone, told him he had choices: apply to a community college, get a job or join the military.

That was the first of March. He broke into my study on the second of March, took my laptop and a handful of thumb drives. Left a note that he'd destroy me.

Strange damn thing, Garrett, he didn't take his car, and I have his driver's license. Hell, I thought he'd be back in a couple of days, bring my things back, and that would be the end of it, so I didn't start to worry until the week was out."

"What on the thumb drives is so valuable to have done serious damage, Sir?"

"All AFOSI personnel with photos, their families, addresses, current assignments, AFOSI operations worldwide, and all *who and how* affiliations with other branches of enforcement agencies. That's all."

"Got it, Sir. We'll do our best."

"Bring back my Paul, Garrett."

* * *

My next call was to Pop. No answer. I called my office. After two rings, *"Gumshoe and Fox,"* came a feminine voice.

"This is Alan Garrett; who's this?"

"Alan! Hi! This is Amy! When are you coming home?"

"Hi, Amy. Not for a while. Is Pop around?"

"No. He's having coffee with Rita at her place. I can take a message, though. I have several for you, too."

"Fax your messages to me at the motel. The number's there somewhere. Fox is in the hospital. I'll be here for a few days more."

"What happened to Fox?"

"To summarize: kidnapped, beaten, escaped from off fishing trawler, swam over two miles, sunburned terribly, in hospital. I'll know more soon. Is job going well?"

"We're making headway. Have found, I think, sixteen more suspicious trusts for you to resolve."

"That's not exactly the agreement. Have Pop call me. Talk to you later." I hung up.

* * *

I toyed around with the idea of calling Rachel. I finally decided, after pouring two fingers of Martell, to make the call.

"Alan! Sweetheart! I've missed you. Are you on your way home? I'll wear your favorite outfit, fix your dinner. Do you need me to pick you up at the airport?"

"Lady, take a breath!" I laughed and took a sip from my glass, "I'm afraid I'm here for a while yet. Fox is in the hospital. I'm on the trail of some bad people. They've stolen documents that could compromise U.S. security around the world."

"Sounds dreadfully serious, Alan. Shouldn't the FBI be involved? Shouldn't you be allowed two weeks vacation to take me fishing, sit under my pergola drinking Martell, skinny dipping in my pool, and enjoying every other thing we could do together?"

"Careful, Rachel. You're being rather racy."

"Ha! You come up with some very interesting ideas when you're with me. I wonder sometimes, am I your only pleasure or are there others?"

"Short answer: no one else . . . longer answer: no one else at the moment . . . but to be sure, Love, hire a good private investigator, but be prepared to spend a lot of money for nothing."

"Then, come home . . . soon, Alan."

* * *

Two more fingers of Martell. I sipped it and let my mind wander to delicious thoughts about the last call when the phone rang. It was the hospital.

It was Nurse Jackie's call telling me to come back at 7 p.m. to spend a few minutes with my friend. The clock on the bedside table confirmed it was yet early . . .

What to do for almost three hours? Eat something, Alan.

I'd been functioning on adrenalin for the last twenty-four hours. I agreed with my stomach, set my fedora on my head and walked out the door. I headed for the cafe on Roosevelt across from the mooring space vacated by the old *Blue Moon*.

Sam and Ernie met me with an invite to join them at their booth . . . *did they never go home*?

"Hi, fellas," I called out as Sam moved over enough for me to sit.

"We heard about your friend," Ernie said.

"Great to hear she's gonna be okay." Sam only nodded.

"I'm going to see her tonight," I said. "Hospital says she's on the mend."

Marge was on shift again. She smiled when she recognized me. "Coffee?" she yelled across the room.

"No thanks, Marge. Just a water and a menu, please," I yelled back. Then I changed my mind. "What's your special tonight?"

She laughed and walked over. "Did you want me to holler the specials all the way across the room? Let's see, we have hamburger steak with your choice of mashed or baked, we have..."

"Stop right there. I'll take that with the baked potato," I smiled. Then a thought struck me.

"Fellas, do either of you remember what the boss looked like? I mean, could you draw his features?"

"Nah," Sam said. "We ain't no artists. We worked as longshoremen until we retired. The last time I drew anything was with color crayons. Ernie, how about you?" he asked his friend.

"I could maybe look at a picture and tell you if it looks like the fella," Ernie replied. "One thing for sure, he wasn't from around here. Educated for sure. Spoke good English. Had an accent."

Marge came with water. "Maybe Marge can draw the guy. She waited on him," Ernie suggested.

"Maybe I can what?"

"Can you draw that fellow the others called the boss the other day?"

"I probably can," Marge laughed, "but right now I'm busy. Your dinner should be ready any moment. Tomorrow morning be okay?"

13

Thursday, October 3. 7 p.m.
Hospital Visit

Jackie met me at the fourth floor elevator. In front of the Sterile Room sat a new security officer, Marian. Jackie introduced us. Then, after donning a white suit and a mask to cover my mouth and nose, we entered.

Fox was sitting up. Her face and neck were covered with a yellowish-colored cream, her arms with cold cotton gauze pads, but she was awake, and less sedated than she had been.

She could neither show facial expression nor mouth more than a few words, but instant recognition and relief showed in her eyes.

"Don't try to speak, Fox. Just get better."

She tried anyway. "Day h-h-h-hab boy. Bad pebul, Gumsh-o-o."

"I know, Fox, But I'm here now, and we'll track them down and get him back."

"M-m-m-my pu-pu-purz, gun, gone. Aw gone, Gumsh-o-o."

"No more talk," I said sternly. She frowned. I continued, "I'm caught up on your capture and escape, I have a couple of leads to follow up on while you're in here, and when you're well enough we'll get the bad pebul."

"F-f-f-f yuu, Gumsh-o-o." She tried to laugh, but ended up coughing. I raised an eyebrow.

"Watch your language, Fox! You're still my subordinate."

"I know about your purse, your gun, your credit card, driver's license, all your other cards. I've taken the liberty to cancel and replace everything replaceable. I'll have your new Beretta tomorrow, FedEx'd down from Miami, your license and carry permit are on their way from Morris--probably at the motel already, and Pop is taking care of your driver's license. So our only worry is will you be healed in time to help me wrap up this case or not."

"Speaking of wrapping up," Jackie said, "I think we should end this session, Mr. Garrett. She'll be stronger tomorrow."

I agreed. "I'll see you tomorrow morning about 7:00, Fox. Get some rest." I blew her a kiss. She gave me a wistful excuse for a smile.

I bid Jackie a good evening, told Marian to keep a sharp lookout and question anyone who looked out of place, then took the elevator down to street level.

As I walked out the door a gentleman with a small bouquet of flowers and a lady on his arm was walking up the sidewalk toward the entrance. When they saw me, I noticed her tug at his arm; they slowed, a quick discussion, and they rerouted to a stretch of sidewalk paralleling the flower beds along the face of the building toward the employee parking lot. *Something's not right, Alan, something's not right!*

I continued to my rented Mustang, and cranked it over. The car sprang to life. I drove out of the lot and headed up Roosevelt. Two blocks away, I pulled the car over, got out and locked it. I then trotted the two blocks back to the hospital.

In the elevator, almost to the fourth floor, I heard the stomach churning exchange of gunfire--a semi-automatic assault rifle and the pop-pop-pop of a hand gun; two separate weapons--then screaming in a foreign language.

My .45 in hand, I exited the fourth floor lobby and almost tripped over Marian. Seven or eight feet away was a man bent over another figure, screaming epithets in a foreign language. A bouquet of flowers was on the floor behind him.

"Drop your weapon," I shouted. Without hesitating, the man pointed his assault rifle and unleashed a burst wildly in my direction; I dropped him with one bullet.

Marian was directly beneath me. I bent down; there was nothing I could do for her. She was dead.

I gave the other two a summary glance. They were no threat. "Bastards!" I said, angrily in their direction.

"Jackie! Are you in here?" I yelled, looking through the observation window and trying the door into the Sterile Room. The door was locked as it should be; the bed was empty and disheveled--like Fox had been dragged or thrown out. I pounded--calling out Fox's name.

Jackie raised her head from behind the bed. "We're okay. Is Pauline there? I need her."

Another nurse's head poked up from behind the nurse's desk. This one, Pauline I assumed, brushed herself off, calmly pushed a button to release the lock on the room across the hall.

"I called the police," she said, as she hurried to the Sterile Room.

More hospital staff and three police officers poured out of the elevator, including the chief, Hector.

"What happened here?" the chief asked. I filled him in on my visit, my return, the gunfire, and my participation.

Jackie and Pauline emerged from the Sterile Room where the nurses had finished readjusting Fox back in the bed.

I poked my head in the door, assured Fox everything was under control, and repeated that I'd see her in the morning. I shut the door and joined the others.

Pauline was confirming my story, adding only a detail or two. An officer was taking photographs of the scene.

Hector looked at the carnage. "Did anyone touch anything?"

"No, Sir," Pauline continued the narration, "it just happened. Marian is leaning against the wall where she fell, the other two are in a heap over there," she pointed. "We haven't even verified that those two are dead."

The chief nodded his head. "Looks like nothing more can be added except identifying these two."

"Check the flowers for a grenade or explosive package of some kind," I instructed one of the other officers, "and be careful picking them up."

He came back with the bouquet. "They're fine." He handed them to Pauline.

Hector called out, "Did anyone call the coroner? We need him over here just to touch the deceased before we take over . . . to keep the books straight.

You folks on staff can go about your business. Garrett, looks like you were right. Stay here, would you? Once the coroner is finished we'll take a look at these two."

He looked down at Marian, shaking his head. Then, breathing out to no one in particular, "Third cop I've lost in six years as chief here in the Keys. Seventeen years in Miami was damn near as safe. I'm getting sick and tired of this shit."

The coroner had already been called and was there within minutes . . . took finger prints and photos of faces, confirmed times of death, although we all knew the time, said his condolences to all present, and was gone.

Hector turned to me. "I don't recognize either one of them. Do you?" I shook my head.

The third officer stood and interrupted, "Hector, there's not a piece of paper between them. No wallets, credit cards . . . nothing. Both equipped with assault rifles."

"Why did you suspect the flowers, Garrett?"

"Professional hit team; I've seen it before, not so much in the states, but in the Philippines. A friendly, loving couple comes visiting. Some bring bouquets or gifts laced with poisons, explosives, but some like this pair bring them as props, nothing more."

"Your involvement was necessary, Garrett, thanks. Go on home. I still have to deal with Marian's husband."

I turned to go. "Have you wondered why they're so keen on silencing my friend, Hector?"

"Sorry, no. Until an hour ago, I thought you were full of bull crap. I humored you by giving your friend a security detail. I was wrong. Do you have any ideas?"

"I have a couple. She either saw too much--possibly that old fishing boat that sank, or perhaps she recognized someone--you know, someone recognizable like, on CNN or ABC."

"Ahhh, sure! Or, perhaps she recognized someone local . . . say, from here in Key West," said Hector.

"Exactly. Good night." I left the hospital and walked slowly up Riverside to the Mustang.

14

Friday, October 4. 7 a.m.
The Hungry Pelican

After a 6 a.m. run with Jennifer I took a quick shower, then called Nell at the hospital. Officer White was on duty. Nell and I discussed the excitement of the night before. She assured me that White, although a bit nervous, was on task.

Liz was getting stronger. Able to say a few words . . . was practicing two words: "people" and another—not so nice, starting with *F*. I had to smile.

I headed for *the Hungry Pelican*. Marge had told me she would have a sketch of the *Boss*. I was counting on it.

The place was buzzing with activity. Every booth and table was occupied, as were most of the stools at the counter. I chose an available one, tipped a mug over and asked for a coffee. Marge was nowhere in sight.

Coffee came. I took a sip. I got a pat on the back. Turned to see Officer Thune. "Hell of a job last night, Garrett." The customer next to me saw the uniform, smiled and offered Thune the seat. He took it. "Hell of a job," he repeated as he sat.

"You and your girl come riding in here; all hell breaks loose; we lose a good cop; you're a hero; your girl swims two miles to safety and is given accolades as a brave lady; yes, sir! hell of a job!"

I turned to look at him, frowning. "You don't like me much, huh? Sorry, Thune. I'm just doing my job . . . following a lead wherever it goes. By the way, can I get that composite description you took from the five nurses a couple of days ago?"

"You got it already--up close and personal, last night, Garrett. Remember? Have a good day, Mr. Private Dick!" He slid off the stool and walked out. A middle-aged woman sat down, smiled and asked for a menu. I did the same. She stuck her hand out and introduced herself as a long-time Florida Keys resident.

"I don't believe I've met you before. I'm Kate Moore. Call me Kate."

"I'm Alan Garrett from California, here on assignment." *Kate Moore, I thought . . . I know that name . . . hmmmm . . . coincidence?*

"Did you hear there was a shooting at the hospital last night?" she asked.

"I was there visiting a patient when it happened, Miss Moore," I said. "Pretty tense for a while, I can tell you." Marge walked up. "Kate, would you please excuse me?" I apologized.

"Good morning, Marge," I said smiling to the waitress as she poured coffee for the counter customers. She smiled back, but continued down the row. She passed me on a return trip, picked up a second carafe and passed me again. "I'll be back," she promised.

I turned back to Miss Moore, "One busy place."

"It's Friday. Everyone in town not working goes out for breakfast on Friday," she said, "just to make weekend plans."

Silly tradition, I thought. *Don't think it's true.*

Marge returned as promised. "More coffee, Kate?" she asked. "And for you, Mr. Detective?"

"Do you have that sketch for me?"

"Aren't you going to order?"

"Sure. Scrambled eggs, hash browns, sour dough toast, real butter, salsa and a sketch."

"I'll take the same," Kate said, "except for the sketch. What's a sketch?"

"I whipped it up for him last night. If he's a gentleman, he'll share," Marge assured her. "Right?" she added, looking at me.

"Of course. One sketch may be more than I can handle." I smiled up at her.

"Smart ass!" she retorted.

"Well, it appears you know Marge," Kate said, turning to me. "And you're a detective? What are you investigating?"

"Trying to find and return a stolen laptop and a few sensitive thumb drives."

"Of a sexual nature no doubt," Kate surmised.

"I wouldn't know. I wasn't told to look at them, just return them," I laughed.

Breakfast came. Marge brought me an extra napkin. It was rolled up with no fork or knife in it--obviously the sketch. I decided to pay close attention to Kate Moore when I unrolled the sketch. I savored a bite of scrambled egg, then said, "Let's take a look at this sketch."

I saw no surprise, no recognition in her eyes as she examined it.

"Like I said, I've been here a long time; don't recognize him," she remarked

"I don't either. Someone in here should, though. He didn't come in until afternoon on the first of October. By the way, I told you what I do. What do you do for a living, Kate?"

"I work down at the marina . . . evenings usually."

"Quite the tragedy, with *The Blue Moon* dragged out and burned, huh?" I didn't wait for her reply. "You were on that night, right?"

"You seem to already have that answer, Mr. Garrett," she returned.

"My job, Ma'am. I get a bit nosey at times. Sorry. You should hear me talk to myself. Sometimes I ask twenty questions, come up with forty answers and only two reasons."

"It's been interesting, Mr. Garrett. Thanks for the company." She scooted down from her stool and walked out the front door, waving at a few other customers.

I took a close look at the sketch. Marge had put in a lot of detail. It was, in fact, really quite good. The next time she came by with the coffee I stopped her.

"Marge, do you and your sketch book have some time to join me today for a visit at the hospital? I'd like you to interview some nurses and my associate, Liz."

"I'm sure I can. It will have to be after 3 p.m. This place goes bonkers on a Friday until mid-afternoon, then everyone goes to the tavern.

"Great! We'll make it four o'clock. Give me your address; I'll pick you up."

"No need. I live across the street from the hospital."

"That's convenient in some ways. Across from the hospital, huh? Didn't I see a cop car parked in that neighborhood yesterday?"

"Yes, my next door neighbor, Gary Thune. What an asshole!"

I laughed as she rolled her eyes and mumbled something unintelligible.

"Bad neighbor, Marge?"

"Oh, most of our cops are the greatest, you know, but this one is such a bullying blowhard, in and out of uniform."

"Sorry, Marge. I'll see you at 4 p.m." She was still mumbling to herself as she walked away, coffee carafe in hand.

I went to the hospital to check in on Liz. She was sleeping soundly. Officer White was sitting as security in front of her room.

"I'm here until 3 p.m." he informed me. "Not sure who Hector will have coming on then. Probably Norm Gornich, another rookie."

We chatted for a few moments, then back to the motel--far too early to call the west coast--perhaps a swim in the motel pool. *Good idea, Alan.*

I found myself the only adult in the pool . . . five preteens, possibly nine to twelve were noisily enjoying the water. There was no parent, no monitor no lifeguard around. I took on the roll.

I pulled a lounge chair near the edge of the pool, and keeping one eye on the kids, I tried to read a book, *A Lad From Sardinia.* I had found it along with some other choices on a shelf in the motel office.

The next three quarters of an hour went quite smoothly . . . the kids had a ball and I relaxed for the first time since coming to Florida.

At 9:15 a.m. two moms came to the gate, plucked up their kids, and it became suddenly all too quiet. I set the book on the chaise and dove into the deep end. So, at 9:45 a.m. while I was enjoying the depths of the motel pool another body slipped underwater at Old Finds Bight.

15

Friday, October 4. 9 a.m.
Barge Fallout

It was an especially muggy Friday morning; air was still . . . the old barge sat motionless on the water, not far from Old Finds Bight, a desolate, marshy waterway not far from Key West. Most of the barge was shaded under a camouflage-tented tarp.

On one end of the barge was a pair of 65 h.p. outboard motors, on the other were wooden crates stacked two or three high. In the center a long wooden table, well used over the years as a fish or crab cleaning station by its various owners.

Strewn here and there along the shoreline were piles of Conch shells four and five feet high; the muddy shoreline was covered with broken pieces of oyster shells, mother-of-pearl shining in the sun.

The table had two benches, one on either side-- now occupied by three women: Joyce, Bette, Claudia, and four men: Antonio, Dario, Nicolas, and Gabriel, all awaiting the Boss.

They were all very good at what they do. One, Antonio, was a private investigator working for the Boss; three: Claudia, Nicolas and Dario were muscle; the last three: Joyce, Bette, and Gabriel were code breakers (they preferred cryptanalysts) --recent hires, vetted by Antonio. They were fluent in English only. The others fluent in Portuguese, Spanish and some English, the investigator variants of several languages. Today they spoke English and broken English.

The first three were steeling themselves for the inevitable ass-chewing one or more would receive when he arrived. Their prisoner should never have escaped.

Following that, they would get on with current business.

"Who else in the local pool?" Nicolas asked. "We can't let this slide much longer. I hear the female in the hospital is almost well enough to speak, and soon well enough to be released."

Claudia spoke up, "We have that California dude nosing around as well. He came back to the hospital! He came back! How the hell he knew I don't understand," she said shaking her head. "It should have been over . . . problem eliminated."

"If it weren't for that woman . . . what is she called?" Gabriel broke in, "Liz?" he continued . . . "if it weren't for Liz, sounds like you would have sailed out of here clean. But perhaps you needed us to decipher your coded message. Maybe your boss won't be so upset when he thinks it through."

A Zodiac approached, the motor cut, the Boss and a companion appeared.

After introductions and cordialities, the Boss began. "First order of business," he said, "we'll be underway at 3 p.m. this afternoon. Set your watches." He looked down at his phone to make sure . . . "It is exactly 9:23 a.m.

Now, let's talk about what has happened in the last four days. We've had to re-adjust our schedule because someone screwed up. Who tied the lady in the hold of that old trawler?"

"I had two of the hands on the yacht do it," Dario said.

"Did you check to make sure you were satisfied with their job?"

"No, Sir. I figured they knew what they were doing."

The Boss walked over and put his hand on Dario's shoulder. "Can't afford to be sloppy." He nodded to Ronaldo. A snub nosed .22 came from Ronaldo's jacket pocket . . . one bullet went through Dario's brain.

The Boss looked up at the rest of those present . . . then to Ronaldo, "Drop him in the Zodiac. We'll strip him naked, dump the body among the alligators."

"You shot him!" screamed Bette. "You shot him!"

Joyce stood. "I didn't sign on to assist murderers. We're supposed to decode information to expose pockets of terrorist cells!"

"Sit!" the Boss demanded. "You will be given your assignments once we get aboard. It's a noble cause. I'm afraid we must be adamant. An order is an order, followed explicitly, otherwise there will be consequences."

Leaving the three code breakers to themselves, the Boss took his crew aside.

"Now, regarding the woman, don't worry about that problem. Ronaldo, here, will take care of her and the dude from California. He assures me no one here will be implicated or involved. He runs his own crew."

"Don't we need to take care of her before we get underway?" Claudia asked. "She's seen all of us, including you, Boss."

"As I said, don't worry. We'll be already underway when Ronaldo visits the hospital. In the meantime I'll make a big deal out of our departure. I'll get hold of the Coast Guard and Harbor Master and give them a revised schedule. *One of our crew will suddenly develop an illness and we must return to South America.*"

"So we're not going to Disney World?" Antonio, the private investigator asked. Around the table everyone laughed, even the Boss.

"Last order of business," the Boss continued. "The boy. The boy is still on a fishing charter, having the time of his life. We have the thumb drives and computer, and he's agreed to sell to us for two million." The Boss laughed, " The fishing is just one perk of the sale.

The sooner these three," he jerked a thumb toward the code breakers, "break the code the sooner they all go over the side. The damn kid claims he found it open and has seen everything on it, including classified information, photos, locations and more.

But what he grabbed is in code; he doesn't even know how to crack it; my team has spent two days so far with no success. It may be worth nothing, but from the way he described it, it should be a gold mine to the right buyer.

Contacting the father is a last resort. But then it turns into kidnapping. U.S. laws frown on kidnapping. A boating accident is far cleaner.

Let's just hope this exercise is worthwhile. Kid's beginning to get on my nerves!" Those around the table saw frustration in their boss for the first time in years.

He looked at his phone. "We'll be going now. Remember 3 p.m." He and Ronaldo boarded the Zodiac. The others sat in silence for a few moments. Finally, Joyce spoke:

"The message is, 'Don't cross the Boss'."

"We've never doubted that, but never so dramatically," Antonio agreed. They all nodded their heads; the Boss was, indeed pissed.

They left by a trail through the bushes to a secluded parking area. A sign behind them said, ***"Private Property. Violators Will Be Prosecuted!"*** From there they meandered in three separate cars through back dirt roads until they reached a graveled unmarked road. That road ended at Highway #1. The three cars turned right, and returned to Key West.

16

Friday, October 4. 1 p.m.
Coast Guard

"Kate Moore. What do you know of Kate Moore, Gumshoe?"

I was sitting on the bed in Room 23, sipping Martell, reliving aloud my morning in *the Hungry Pelican.*

"Kate seemed to be on a reconnaissance mission. Smelled like it, anyway. Why has this Buck Watters, the real Harbor Master, not made an appearance . . . sound me out for himself?"

"There can be only one Harbor Master, so Kate evidently works as assistant Harbor Master to him in the evenings; what does she do days?"

Just thinking out loud, Gumshoe. I took another sip. *You're probably full of shit,* I thought silently. *Maybe a trip to see the Coast Guard is in order.* I grabbed my fedora and a minute later I was heading for the Coast Guard detachment in Key West.

A young lady was at the desk, dressed in her whites.

"May I help you?"

"I'm looking for one of the officers that was involved in overseeing *The Blue Moon* disaster," I said, removing my fedora. "Perhaps one is available . . . Bill or Fernando?"

"I'll check. That's where the three people were found shot, right? Are you the lady's friend? The one in the hospital?"

"Sadly, that's right," I smiled.

A few minutes later Fernando opened a door and ushered me into an inner office. Henry appeared moments later bringing a carafe of coffee and mugs.

After handshakes and a sip of coffee *I cut to the chase* as they say.

"I'm sure you heard about the shooting at the hospital last night; that was, of course, an attempt on my assistant. Someone is trying to shut her up. She knows something, has seen someone, can identify a prominent local figure involved in criminal activity, something. I'm not sure, but I'll guarantee it involves something of a marine nature, something the Coast Guard should be investigating. Do you agree?"

"It's too early to tell, Garrett," Henry exclaimed. "*The Blue Moon* incident could be a separate incident altogether. We, along with the police, are investigating the shooting deaths on the trawler, but there's not much to go on."

I scowled, "Come on fellas! Craft big enough to pull her off her moorings are few and far between! You and the Harbor Master must have a list, even an accounting of tugs or working trawlers that move in and out of these waters."

Fernando, after a couple of minutes of further discussion, said, "Here's what we'll do. We'll put together a list of heavy craft that harbor here, the marina and berth of each, and get an accounting of their movements on October one. Does that satisfy you?"

"For now, yes, so long as I receive a copy of that report," I smiled. "Oh, by the way. Three more questions: One, where does Buck Watters hang his hat? Two, have you ever checked further on that Brazilian yacht, *Bordereau*? and Three," I said, unfolding Marge's sketch, "does this fellow look familiar?"

"Strange you should concern yourself with that yacht, Garrett." Henry frowned, He stared at the sketch for a moment, then looked away . . . but I noticed . . . "*Bordereau* is leaving us just today on her way home. The pilot and another crew member were in an hour ago to let us know. They have had to change their itinerary due to an illness on board."

So, I thought, *the Bordereau is leaving us; if Paul is on that boat I need to know where he's going. I need to track that yacht!*

I had two GPS trackers in my glove compartment; how to place them on the yacht may prove a challenge, but I'll try.

"Yes," Fernando was saying, "you can probably catch Buck there any time in the next half hour. He usually checks out foreign vessels if they are leaving after a visit of some duration. We sent one of our guys there as well. I think Bill is there. You met Bill, right?"

"Yes. Thanks, fellas," I said, looking at the time. "Oh! and the sketch?"

"Could be anybody," Henry laughed.

"Yes, I suppose," I agreed.

We shook hands. "Look forward to that list." I returned my fedora to my head, said goodbye to the young lady at the front desk and walked out.

Casual group if ever I met one, I thought. *And at least one of them is a liar!*

17

Friday, October 4. 2 p.m.
Buck Watters

Friday afternoon–still muggy and a bit overcast. A lot of foot traffic met me as tired fishermen were coming back from a day on the water in their boats . . . I was headed out to the end of the pier where the *Bordereau* lay tied.

I followed a pair of males dressed in work clothes -- the picture in my mind put the word *"Sailor"* in rectangular boxes above their heads as they swaggered the length of the pier. Funny how the mind works. Maybe just mine.

As we walked, I became more and more sure they were part of the *Bordereau* crew. I caught up with them, GPS tracker in my hand

"Excuse me fellows. Are you part of the crew of yonder yacht?" I asked, pointing at the craft in the end berth.

Both stopped and looked at me blankly. I tried again, this time in Spanish. Big smiles came back at me. "Ah, Si, Señor," one of them replied, "She is our boat--*Bordereau,* she is our boat! Just Juan and me." He slapped his friend, Juan on the back; they both hooted with laughter. I put an arm around each of them, dropping the tracker in Juan's pocket as I did.

"And your name is?"

"Tomas, Señor."

"Tomas and Juan, you boys take good care of that boat. My name is Garrett."

I walked with them a few steps, laughing, then wished them a good trip and retreated.

These two are harmless enough, I thought. *Maybe I have the wrong idea about the Bordereau. Maybe my gut feeling has really gone off the rails this time. The GPS tracker? No big loss if it didn't pan out.*

Four others passed me on their way to the yacht, making a total of six including two women.

Just as I approached the gangway, two gentlemen were shaking hands with, I assumed, the yacht's captain . . . the fellow I had seen two nights before. One of the two was Bill from the Coast Guard, the other, a very rotund gentleman in a shirt and white shorts . . . *must be Buck Watters,* I thought. *Hasn't missed very many meals in his maybe 40-45 years. Looked a bit like a cartoon character . . . Little Lulu's friend, Tubby maybe, or perhaps Popeye's bud, Wimpy . . . oh, stop! Alan!*

All the original feelings of evil came bounding back. I waited. Now was not the time. I had no "*Welcome aboard!*" from the Yacht. I couldn't call out, "*Permission to come aboard?*" . . . that would draw a response, "*Who are you, and why?*"

"*Uh, well Sir, you see, I'm a private detective, and I, uh, I wanted to snoop around your yacht because I suspect something is, uh, not quite right.*"

So I waited. Besides, I had Bill and Buck to talk with for a few minutes if they don't snub my charismatic charm, perhaps join me for a donut and coffee at a kiosk I had passed on the pier.

Bill recognized me at once. With a broad smile he introduced me to Buck.

"Good afternoon. I came down here hoping I'd run into you," I said.

"Oh, we know," Bill laughed. "Henry called and told us to look for you. What's up?"

"I just want to clear some things up in my mind.Could we stop at that kiosk a way down the pier for a coffee and chat for a moment?"

"I'm not sure I ha . . ." Bill was interrupted by Buck.

"Ginny's?" Absolutely! Ginny makes the best apple fritters in Key West. We have time, right, Bill?"

"Sure."

Coffee and donut at the table--Bill asked, "How can we help you, Mr. Garrett?"

"Alan, please. I'm very curious about the yacht you were just on. Captain Whats-his-name, I understand, changed travel plans because of an illness on board."

"That's correct. It's Captain Bosignion, by the way. Austrian. Nice fella. Too bad, too," Buck said. "They were planning to visit Miami, and even take a van up to Disney World for all on board. Bosignion was even looking forward to the day at Disney. Ha!" Buck said, "He ended up giving us all his tickets."

He pulled an envelope from his checkered

shirt pocket and spread ten entry tickets on the table. "Want tickets for Disney World, Alan?"

"Ha! No," I laughed. "Did you check the sick fellow to verify?"

"No. He was in sick bay."

"Do you have the total number of persons on board. Check their passports and such?"

"Of course!" There are ten. Why the third degree, Alan?" Bill asked.

"Six crew members were just ahead of me, boarding. I didn't see any passports produced as they went up the gangway. You were wishing the Captain a *bon voyage* at the time."

"They showed them as they passed, smart ass!" Bill retorted. "You have a piss-poor manner about you, Mr. Garrett. I think we're done here."

"I only have one more questio..."

"Screw you, Garrett!" Buck dropped his last bite of apple fritter on the table, picked up the ten tickets and followed Bill off the pier.

I have that effect on some people . . . but to leave a bite of apple fritter?

* * *

I sat at the table there at Ginny's, tossed some small bits of apple fritter to the starlings and sparrows that came winging in to mooch, and watched as six more people–three women, three men–boarded the *Bordereau.* These were not dressed in scrubs as the first six I had seen. These were more hardened, more like soldiers. I was now sure. I had the right target.

The GPS tracker I had dropped in Juan's pocket was not in vain!

18

Friday, October 4. 3 p.m.
An Accident On Highway #1

The *Bordereau* embarked right on schedule--3 p.m. I stayed at my kiosk work station to photograph and document every new addition to those on board . . . I counted thirteen before she pulled up anchor. There were probably more.

I had almost an hour before meeting Marge at the front desk of the hospital; might as well go early.

Maybe a quick trip to the cafeteria for a sandwich, Alan. Then I thought of Buck Watters and cartoon frames of Tubby . . . *ummmm, Don't go there, Gumshoe* . . . but I smiled . . . *you don't need a sandwich anyway.*

Instead, I walked to the front desk, checked in, and took the elevator to the fourth floor. Nell greeted me with a big smile. Another nurse, Connie, was sitting behind the desk, and a new security officer was sitting in the chair across the hall. Nell introduced me to Norm Gornich, then gave me the latest on Liz.

"She's doing so much better, Mr. Garrett. You'll be pleased. But right now she's asleep."

"I have Marge from the *Hungry Pelican* coming at 4 p.m. to get a description--make a sketch of that first gunman. You'll be here, right? Can you make sure she's awake by then?"

"Yes to both questions. Not a problem. In fact I'll be waking her just before Kate comes on at four."

"Kate?" Is this Kate Moore?"

"Yes. She worked here full-time for three years, but eight months ago Key West needed an evening Harbor Master, she passed a written exam, then an oral exam with Buck Watters. He hired her over a few other applicants. She's on leave from the hospital except Fridays. Fridays are tough here in the Keys; seems we always need more staff."

So, I asked myself, *does this have something to do with my morning encounter with Kate Moore? Another coincidence?*

"Oh! Nice! I just met her this morning," I said. "So, she's a nurse," I mused. "Huh!"

"Small town," Nell laughed.

"Will she be taking care of Liz in the Sterile Room?" I asked.

"Sure. As I told you before, Mr. Garrett, every member on staff is qualified and trained to deal with disaster. Don't forget, this is hurricane country. Kate has proven as good as any of us."

Nell's phone rang. I left her, pushed an office chair across the hall, and sat to have a chat with Norm. Thirty-one, single, a recent graduate of the Miami police academy. His first assignment: five months in Fort Lauderdale, then transferred two weeks ago to Key West.

"Keep your eyes and ears open this afternoon, Norm. You heard what happened here last night. Whoever is trying to shut the young lady's mouth will try again, and with more determination. I may have to make some adjustments."

"What do you mean, adjustments?"

"I'll let you know in a few minutes. Right now, I'd like to speak with Nell and perhaps the doctor on site."

Across the aisle, Nell set the phone down, a worried look on her face. She looked first at Connie, then at Norm and me.

"A wreck out on Highway #1," she said, her voice strained, "one of our high school buses; no other vehicle involved. Hector says we'd better call in reinforcements. He says the bus rolled over, driver is dead, some serious injuries."

"That's bad news, Nell. I'm sorry," I said. "I'll stick around here. Who else is on this floor that I should look in on?"

"You're not looking in on anyone, Mr. Garrett," Nell assured me, with a chuckle. "Connie will stay here until we get a fix on the incoming injured. Then we will divide the chores up and call off-duty personnel as needed. I'll be right back. I'm going to emergency admitting." She scurried into the open elevator.

"Connie," I turned to the young nurse, "are there any vacant rooms on this floor?"

"Oh, sure. This floor has 12 rooms, reserved for extreme physical injury only: loss of limb-- Perhaps through alligator bite; burn victims-- perhaps a boat fire, or as in your friend's case, severe sun exposure; or trauma--a serious gunshot wound . . . come to think of it, we've only had one of those in the last four years . . . until last night."

"That's fine," I smiled, "but are there any vacant rooms?"

"All of them, Mr. Garrett, except for your friend's."

"Then, we're going to move Liz," I said. "Open her room for me, and show me how to unlock her wheels. We'll roll her into a different room."

Both Connie and Norm shook their heads but helped me push Liz down the hall from the Sterile Room to Room #411, at the far end. We took that bed and rolled it to the Sterile Room, then bulked up the bed with pillows to appear occupied.

"Should I move down the hall, Mr. Garrett?" Norm asked.

"No!" I said, frowning. "That would defeat any subterfuge we are attempting."

"You think there will be another attempt on her life?" Connie asked, understanding what just happened.

"I do."

I was about to go back to Room #411 when my phone rang. I thought it was probably Pop. I glanced at it. I was wrong. It was Hector.

"Garrett, we have a problem."

"What's up, Hector?" I asked. "Are we talking about the bus accident?"

"No accident, Garrett," Hector assured me. "Murder."

19

Friday, October 4. 3:30 p.m.
Bus Accident

"What?" I asked, incredulously. "How? Who?"

"Bus driver. Some kids on the bus verified. A black sedan pulled up alongside, driver smiled, motioned for Chuck to open his window. When he did, driver of black sedan opened up with an assault rifle, shot Chuck just as the bus was rounding a curve. The bus flipped, the sedan sped off."

"It's Friday, Chief. Where were kids going on a bus? A football team?"

"No, they're the pride of the Keys . . . the debate team. On their way to Miami for a competition. The event starts at 7 p.m."

"Damn!" I said. "I'm so sorry. But, why call me, Hector?"

"Because I think it may be a ruse; a ruse to scramble the hospital staff for the emergency that it is, and get rid of your girl in the middle of the chaos. I'm on my way there now, but consider this call as a heads up, Garrett."

"Thanks, Hector." I hung up.

"Connie, I want you to take the elevator to assist Nell and the other staff with the incoming injured. Norm and I will be just fine up here. Don't say anything about moving Liz, just say that she's sleeping soundly and you can be more help down there."

Connie shrugged her shoulders. "If you're sure," she said, and left.

When the elevator door closed I told Norm to leave the chair where it was, but join me behind the nurse's station. Ten minutes passed . . . when the door finally opened, Hector appeared, along with officer Thune and Nell. The Chief was first to speak.

"Everything okay up here? Thank God. Maybe I was wrong, Garrett. Maybe the shooting on the highway is unrelated to your lady . . . but a shooting on one of our school buses," Hector shook his head, "that should never happen here in the Keys."

"What's the extent of the injuries?" I asked.

Nell took over. "There are three with facial and neck lacerations—one of those in critical condition—she'll be brought up here once the doctors have made an assessment and initial treatment; two have broken arms; one, a broken collarbone; the other four aboard were treated for cuts and sprains and released."

Hector and Thune turned to go, satisfied that the floor seemed secure enough.

"Stay vigilant, Norm," the chief said to his young rookie. The elevator doors closed and they were gone.

Nell looked at me and frowned. "I understand you, of your own accord, pulled Liz out of the Sterile Room and put her down the hall. You have no right to do that, Mr. Garrett!"

"How did you hear that news?" I asked nonchalantly.

"The nurses had a meeting while in Triage. Connie mentioned it. Now, you get that patient back in the Sterile Room right now!" she demanded.

"I thought Kate was coming on shift. Why are you back up here?" I asked, half in jest, half in irritation.

Fire suddenly shot out of her eyes. "I run this floor, Mr. Garrett! You don't!"

"Oh, just go home, Nell. I have a gut feeling the afternoon will not end pleasantly. If I'm wrong, I'll move her out of the room she's in. I promise."

"Macho bastard!" Nell shouted. "You're the reason I'm not married!" She strode down the hall and entered Room #411 as Norm and I stood and watched. Seconds later she had somehow managed to prop the door open, and the foot of the bed emerged.

At that moment the elevator doors opened. Kate Moore was pushed into the hall, a burly arm around her neck. The man behind her was forcing a small caliber revolver with suppressor against her temple. European, thirties, experienced, good-looking, scary.

"Gentlemen," he smiled, "your guns on the floor, please." We complied.

"I think I'll do the lady first," he remarked casually. "Which room is the Sterile Room?"

Our intruder released his hold on Kate. She nodded her head toward the Sterile Room. "The one by the chair," she said.

Down the hall I saw the bed pulled silently back into Room #411, then to my surprise, I saw Nell emerge from the room, slam the door, and race for the stairwell. That diversion was enough for me to slide along the floor, pick up my .45 and put two shots into the hit-man as he stood confused in choosing targets . . . he made the wrong choice. Both my shots found their mark. He lay in a pool of blood.

"Cuff her," I told Norm.

"Sir?" he asked, "cuff who?"

"The nurse!"

"But the guy had a gun to her head, Sir. She's a victim."

"Trust me, Norm, she's not a victim. Now cuff her, then check her purse and pockets," I advised him.

I kept my gun on Kate while Norm complied. She had no gun, but in her purse he discovered two covered syringes, approximately 2 ml of an unknown fluid in each.

While we were wrapping up, Hector accompanied by Nell, showed himself back at the elevator car.

"This is the fellow, huh? Good work, both of you."

Nell saw Kate's handcuffs. "Kate! Are you involved? Impossible!" She looked from Norm to me . . . "She's a nurse! Release her."

"Test these," I handed Nell the syringes. "If they're sedatives or harmless medication, I'll have her released."

"No, if they're not dangerous, I'll release her," Hector declared. "Now take the syringes to the lab and test them."

"No need," Kate blurted out. "Pentobarbital. They thought it the best, because it is not readily available in hospitals."

"Who is *they*, Miss?" Hector asked.

"I don't know, I swear. I just get instructions in letters, along with cash for following the last set of instructions."

"What kind of instructions?"

"Look the other way when a vessel comes in, mostly."

"Who's your friend?" I asked. "I've checked his pockets--found nothing, not even a cell phone."

"That's Manny, the Boss's main hit-man. When all else fails, this guy gets sent in."

"The Boss? who's the Boss?"

"I don't know."

Hector called the coroner; Norm escorted Kate to jail. The fireworks were over.

I opened Room #411. No Liz. I walked into the room. "Fox," I whispered, "Fox, come out, come out wherever you are."

"Gumshoe, do we have Paul yet?" She was sitting on the floor. "Get me out of here, and let's go grab him, then get the hell out of Florida."

"Fox, we don't even know where he is," I laughed, as I pulled her up.

"But he'll be easy to find. I looked on a map, Gumshoe. The whole of the Keys is only one half inch wide and seven inches long."

I yelled at Nell. She came down the hall.

"Nell, I'm pulling Liz out now. Give me some of that salve you use on her. Enough for a couple of days. I'll take care of her."

"You shouldn't. It's not safe for her."

"It's not safe? We've figured in a cop and a bus driver getting killed, several youngsters injured and three young gangsters found dead on *The Blue Moon* This is not over, Nell. Not by any means. I'm taking her out of here tonight."

Fox wrapped herself in the hospital gown. Nell stopped trying to talk me out of it. Instead, she walked with Fox and me to the elevator.

"Wait there a moment; I'll get salve." She was back in moments and handed me two large tubes of lotion.

"I'm so sorry I doubted you, Mr. Garrett," she said as Fox and I entered the elevator. "You have an extraordinary sense of intuition. Tell me, when did you begin to suspect Kate?"

I pushed the button for the first floor lobby. "Just after I ruled you out, Nell," I answered, dryly.

20

Saturday, October 5.
Overnight Changes

I made sure Fox was comfortable in our room. She was recovered and limber enough to apply the salve herself.

"I'm fine, Gumshoe," she said, raising an eyebrow, "but there's only one bed in here. You're not thinking of . . . well, you know, are you?"

"Absolutely not!" I said emphatically.

"Wow, Bossman, that was rather abrupt. You should have hesitated a few seconds . . . make a girl feel better about herself . . . and then maybe something like, 'Oh, Fox, I don't think so.'"

"I'm leaving now," I laughed, and headed to the motel office to discuss a change of rooms, perhaps adjoining rooms.

Jennifer's mom was behind the desk. "Mr. Garrett. You do know how to upset a town, I'll say that much for you."

I'd like to change to two adjoining rooms if available," I said "Otherwise, two next to each other."

"Best I can do is a suite with two bedrooms. Won't be available until tomorrow afternoon. Will that work?"

"Perfect. Tonight I sleep on the floor."

"You'll need some extra towels. By the way, Marvin is doing just fine."

"Marvin? You mean Munch? What's with him?" I asked.

"He was in the bus rollover. Jennifer didn't tell you? Face is all cut up and broken collar bone."

"I'm so sorry. No, I haven't seen her since this morning's run. I'll see her again tomorrow morning."

Fox was sitting up in the kingsize bed, three pillows behind her. She had a Martell in her hand, and a second on the bedside table beside her.

"I've been snooping," she raised her glass. "Ahh, good! You brought more towels.You get the floor. There's an extra pillow in the closet. It's been a tough day for me, all that shooting and jostling in the hospital. Goodnight, Gumshoe."

I don't think she took a breath. She was asleep in minutes.

I turned out the lamp on her side of the bed, and turned on the other one. Then I took my shoes off sat on the bed and opened the book I had been reading . . . the one about a young fella on the Mediterranean Sea.

An hour later I put the book down, took a long shower, found the pillow, and a nice spot on the carpet to spend the night.

*   *   *

The bus shooting and second hospital shooting--all within two days--brought outrage from most of the 28,000 citizens of the quiet community. The five shootings brought reporters from major newspapers all over Monroe and Dade Counties. They swarmed the Key West police department, the hospital personnel, and hearing that a female assistant Harbor Master was arrested, they spent considerable time interviewing Buck Watters and the Coast Guard.

Between the hospital and police department staffs, Liz's privacy--identity and location--was kept secure, but my identity couldn't be kept private. I was the shooter of two thugs in the hospital. The media wanted to know who and why, and more importantly, why was I, a private investigator from California involved?

* * *

It was 7:30 a.m. Saturday morning. Jennifer and I had finished our 6 a.m. run, then back to the motel to change clothes. While we were running I asked Jennifer to meet with Liz and me for lunch at the motel. She agreed.

Next I went to *The Hungry Pelican* for breakfast and a "to go" order for Liz. That's where the media caught up with me . . . in *The Hungry Pelican.*

First entering was a cameraman with WPLG - Miami on the side of his shoulder-mounted camera. I was at the bar relishing my first bite of steak on a steak'n eggs platter when I noticed others sitting at breakfast whispering about the newcomer. I turned to look.

A lady reporter with the mic and fanny pack was following the cameraman through the doors.

"Oh, crap!"

I must have mumbled too loudly. The waiter pouring coffee(Marge has Saturdays off--his name tag said Joe) stopped and questioned my breakfast.

The lady reporter came directly toward me.

"Mr. Garrett? Alan Garrett?" she asked.

"That's me," I acknowledged. She was very pretty, late twenties, and of course, blond. *(reporters are always young, pretty and blond . . . well, maybe not Mike Wallace . . . choose a different career path if you don't fit that profile)* I volunteered nothing more to this one; I figured she could do all the talking.

I turned back to Joe, holding out my coffee mug, "Nothing to do with the breakfast, Joe, just the environment," I smiled at him. He nodded.

"Mr. Garrett," the lady continued, "we'd like to talk to you about the two men you killed in the hospital."

"The police have my deposition," I frowned. "All above board. Talk to them." I went back to my eggs and steak.

"Who's the lady, Mr. Garrett?"

I swung the stool back around. "A private investigator." Before I could swing around again she had another question.

"Aren't you also a private investigator?"

"Yes, Ma'am."

"What are you and the lady doing in south Florida?"

"Private investigating, Ma'am."

"Where is the lady now?"

"Safe."

"She's in hiding? Is she in danger?"

"She's safe," I repeated.

"What are you investigating down here that gets five people killed?"

"That's the part of our investigating that remains private, Ma'am. Otherwise we'd be reporters." I smiled.

The entire restaurant burst out laughing. The lady and the cameraman walked out.

* * *

Back in the motel room I tied the GPS tracker into one of our laptops. Fox would monitor its movements.

21

Saturday, October 5.
Cleaning House

Hector had been beleaguered all morning long by the press. His patience was growing thin. When I dropped in unannounced at 9:30 a.m. he was actually pleased to see me.

"Alan, why didn't you wait until I was on vacation? I always take two weeks around Thanksgiving. Coffee?" He pressed a button. "Two coffees, please, Sergeant, and no more visitors this morning." Three or four minutes later officer Thune walked in with three cups of coffee and seated himself next to me across from Hector.

"I wanted to talk with you as well, so when I overheard your request I took over from the desk sergeant," he explained. "I hope that's okay."

"Sure," Hector said, smiling.

"No problem," I agreed. "In fact I have somewhere else to be . . . just remembered." I stood to go. "I'll catch you later, Hector."

"Wait!" Hector protested. "You just sat down!"

"I'll see you before Thanksgiving," I said and walked out without touching the coffee. I was a half block away, still smiling at the shocked look on Thune's face. *Asshole!* I'm sure there was a small discussion still going on in Hector's office.

Buck Watters was on my list of interviews this morning; now is a good time. He had two places to hang his hat, one was a suite of offices on Roosevelt complete with front-end secretary/clerk, the other was a shack at the main marina where he conducted face to face meetings with, usually, incoming and outgoing international vessels, checking passports against crew, duration of trip, cargo, destination, et-cetera.

I called his cell phone . . . no answer.

Now's the time to flip a coin--Roosevelt or Marina?" Roosevelt won the toss. I dialed the land line . . . no answer. Where was his clerk? I dialed Hector.

"Hector," I started . . .

"What the hell was that all about?" he started.

"No time! Send Thune or someone to Buck's Roosevelt address; I'm on my way to the marina!" I slammed the phone down and hopped into my Mustang. The marina wasn't far away. I ran to his shack, midway up the pier, poked my head in . . . nothing.

I walked to the end of the main pier, thinking about my afternoon. Lunch with Liz and Jennifer was already scheduled . . . with an ulterior motive. *What next, Gumshoe? Ahh! Then perhaps a visit to the Coast Guard offices. They should have that list I had asked for. The one Fernando promised:* "Here's what we'll do. We'll put together a list of heavy craft that harbor here, and get an accounting of their movements on October one."

My thoughts took shape audibly: "I'll take Fox with me if she's well enough." I nodded my head as I walked, oblivious to the few boaters on the pier, most of whom were gawking as I passed by. "She'll enjoy being free, after being cooped up."

I stopped to call Henry to ask about the list.

"Any time after 2 p.m," he assured me, "the report will be ready."

A few minutes later Hector called back. "Watters is dead; his clerk is dead. Damn! How did you know, Garrett?"

"Buck was dirty," I said. "He was also a weak link. Someone knew he'd spill the beans sooner or later. That *someone* quieted him. Thank God the town has you as chief. Just be careful."

"How do you know all this after only three days, Garrett?"

"Twenty years of chasing after the same type, Hector. Just be careful," I repeated.

Time for a decision . . . "Pizza or Chicken?" I considered both, then tossed a coin. Turns out, it's three cheeseburgers, with fries and shakes from *the Hungry Pelican.*

22

Saturday, October 5.
Ulterior Motives

I stopped in at the motel office. Jennifer was waiting for me, all excited. "What's the deal, Alan?"

"Let's just go have lunch with Fox. I have a few ideas I'd like to run by you, but let's have lunch first."

"Oh, by the way, Alan, I have a package for you. Comes from Miami."

"Oh! Let me see it."

The brown kraft-wrapped package was addressed to me from Worldwide Tactical. I smiled. "Liz will be pleased," I said.

"Another thing, Alan," Jennifer continued, handing me a key card. "Your new room. Fox is already there. The suite has a kitchenette, so you can cook your own breakfasts. *The Chelsea House* aims to please," she laughed.

"And we're grateful. Let's have lunch," I said.

* * *

I handed Fox the package that had come from Miami. She opened it. "A new Beretta-92! Thanks,

Bossman! I was afraid I'd be naked until we returned to Manhattan Beach!"

"Stick with me, Kid. You'll never be naked!" . . . I couldn't help myself.

Jennifer laughed. "So, what's this big mystery you want to discuss with me?"

"Do I smell burgers with fries? I'm starving!" Fox interrupted. "Let's eat, then you can talk!"

Fox was almost back to her old self. We enjoyed our lunch with very little conversation other than comparing fries from *The Hungry Pelican* to fresh McDonalds' fries, how onions make a good hamburger and . . . passing her new Beretta around, discussing how I was able to order and have it delivered via parcel post, and so rapidly.

"I have connections," was my only response. "Lunch is over," I announced, wiping my hands on my napkin. "First order of business is a trip to the Coast Guard, I have an appointment at 2 p.m.– open invite to both of you. You well enough, Fox?"

"Sure, Bossman, a hundred percent except for the scars on my wrists and my slow-healing forehead."

"You sure it's just your forehead or the stuff inside, Fox? Why did you allow yourself to be discovered?"

"I'm sorry, Bossman. It won't happen again."

"Damn right it won't!" I may have been a bit harsh. "But," I gave her a hug, "glad you're okay."

"It won't, Gumshoe, I promise," she returned the hug . . . in fact, clung to me for a few extra milliseconds.

"So, where's our yacht today, Fox?"

"She's still in port in Havana, Gumshoe. Beginning to think they found your tracker and tossed it in the harbor."

"Nah, Fox. Jacket of a hard-working sailor. He probably hung it on a peg in the boiler room, maybe even tossed it in a drawer if he found it."

Turning to our hostess I said, "Jennifer, I'm going to clue you in on a couple of things that have happened in the last two days. Just yesterday the Port lost its part-time Harbor Master and about an hour ago Buck Watters and his clerk were shot to death in his office."

"Oh! That's awful!" Jennifer exclaimed. "Who shot them?"

"Hector is working on it, Coast Guard is bound to investigate since the Harbor Master is under their purview and," I assured her, "we will be involved to the extent that it falls within our scope of investigating the whereabouts of Paul Maggorie."

"So, why are you cluing me in?" Jennifer asked.

"You're considering criminology, right? The Keys are going to need a new Harbor Master . . . not that a person can just waltz into the Coast Guard offices and present him or herself. But who knows?

Introduce yourself, tell them you're changing majors to criminology. I think you'll have a shot in a few months with the right connections: Coast Guard, Hector, perhaps me . . . just something to consider, Jen."

"You have my future all planned, do you, Gumshoe?" she laughed. "It is something, though. And I was seriously considering police work. But

Harbor master? I don't know . . . but I'll think on it.

Buck was a sham as a Harbor Master. I'm surprised he lasted as long as he did; but I am sorry he's dead. His clerk was Lucy. She's dead, too?"

"Yes."

"Too bad."

"Shall we go?" Fox asked. "I haven't seen much of Key West other than water, the restaurant and the motel room."

* * *

The Coast Guard Station is situated at the end of Front Street, northwest end of the main town.

"What a neat, old building!" Liz blurted out. "It's really old, huh?"

"Yes," Jennifer replied. "We studied it in school. I can tell you who built it, what it's made of, and some of the historical anecdotes old-timers have passed down.

It was built in 1856 as a munitions depot for the Union Troops blockading the Southern forces from obtaining supplies during the Civil War. You wouldn't think so, but it was also a coal storage facility as maritime transport was changing from sail to steam."

"Aren't you sorry you asked?" I laughed, glancing at Liz.

"No! Not at all!" Fox glared back at me. "It looks big enough to house an army . . . or navy. I'm surprised it wasn't turned into a grand hotel."

"That's funny, because as a matter of fact, during the war the Union Troops had what was called the West Indies Blockade Squadron headquartered in the building. Historians have credited that squadron with shortening the war and saving countless lives of both Union and Rebel troops by their efforts.

Then after the war it became Administration Headquarters for the U.S. Navy, after that as District Headquarters for the U.S.Lighthouse Service, and finally in 1939 the Coast Guard took it over as District Headquarters. The Federal Government decided it belongs to the list of Historical Buildings, and registered it as Marker #111 in 1973."

"Wow!" Fox exclaimed, "thanks for that short history lesson. I would never have known any of this. Isn't this interesting, Gumshoe? We're parked in front of a building that figured prominently in shortening the Civil War, and virtually an unknown chapter in the historical record to most Americans. Huh, the West Indies Blockade Squadron--never heard of them."

"It is interesting. Thanks, Jennifer . . ." I was about to say something profound, but Liz interrupted, sarcasm dripping from each word:

"It is interesting. Thanks, Jennifer! Where's the enthusiasm, zest, delight? Gumshoe?"

Jennifer was now laughing. "Honestly, you two sound like an old, married couple. Are you sure you're just two private eyes working together?"

As if on cue a resounding, "We're sure!"

It was 2:15 p.m. "Ready to go in?" I asked.

Jennifer and I walked straight to the front entrance; Liz was moving very slowly, still taken by the old, plaster-coated brick structure and the untold stories it held.

The same young lady in her whites greeted us with the same exuberance as before. "Good day, Mr. Garrett. And you, Miss, I've seen you in town, but we haven't met."

"Jennifer Little, Ma'am, just call me Jen."

Liz walked through the door just then. "I'm with them. I'm Fox," she offered her hand.

"Ensign Brady, Miss Fox," she said shaking the hand Liz offered. "Three of you. The Commander is expecting you." She led us to the conference room where I saw three familiar faces in white uniforms on one side of the table, facing us. "There's water in there. Any coffees?" she asked.

We all declined. "Water will be fine, Ensign Brady," I answered.

We walked in and seated ourselves--I sat between the two ladies.

There was another young lady in the room I hadn't seen before. Henry introduced her as Lieutenant Commander Helen Martaise, a new transfer to Key West.

Continuing around the table each of us introduced ourselves. Halfway through the introductions, Fox clutched my knee.

Henry continued. "We'll make this a formal meeting, as not much has happened in the Key West environs until recently. More has happened in the past week of a maritime nature than we've seen since," he hesitated . . .

"The Civil War, Sir?" Fox broke in. Everyone laughed. *God bless her*, I thought. *She's back!*

"Not quite, Miss Fox," Henry continued, smiling, "but a long time. You're the young lady who was kidnapped, escaped, and has been hospitalized until recently aren't you? Seems you've been the center of attention for some very evil people."

Fox clutched my leg again as she spoke. "Yes, so it seems. And it seems the evil is still present . . . even in this room, Sir." She clutched tighter.

I looked at Henry, then around the room as smiles disappeared, replaced by unease.

"Would you excuse us a moment, Sir?" Not waiting for an answer I pulled Fox's chair back for her and we walked into the hallway.

"It's him, Bossman. It's him! Dial your police friend."

I complied. As the phone rang I asked, "Who, Fox? The Commander?"

"No. The Chief Warrant Officer, Hendricks."

"You mean Bill? Is he the Boss?"

Hector came on the line. He listened on the speaker as Liz explained to me . . .

"No, he's not the Boss, but he was on *The Blue Moon* that night. And yes, it's the Chief Warrant Officer Bill. He was instructing the crew that threw me in the fish hold. The minute I saw him, I thought, *'wow, that's that guy!'*, but he was wearing street clothes Tuesday night so I sort of doubted myself; but just now, when he introduced himself, his voice was the last nail in his coffin."

"You're sure, then I'm sure. Let's take him down, Partner!"

I heard Hector say, "On my way!" as Liz said, "Partner? Now, I'm a partner?"

"Poor choice of words. I meant *Subordinate,* Fox."

We walked back in. Eyes followed us as we sat back down.

"Is everything alright?" Henry asked.

Liz poured herself a glass of water. "It will be soon," she announced. "We called Hector; he'll be joining us in a few minutes."

"Okkkaaay," Henry said shaking his head and raising an eyebrow, "We'll go on, pretending you're not here, Miss Fox.

Detective Garrett, we have the list you asked for. Hendricks, I believe you have that report, right?"

"Yes, I have it right . . . ooops, I must have left it on my desk. I'll be right back, Sir." He walked out.

I spoke up, "Sir, he won't be returning."

"What, Garrett? Why?"

"He was one of the culprits on *The Blue Moon* last Tuesday night."

"No! . . . Shit! Shouldn't we be going after him?"

"He can't get far, Sir, only one road out, and of course, The Coast Guard watches over our waterways. And besides, I continued, "Hector probably already has him in custody."

I was right. A knock on the conference door. Ensign Brady poked her head in. "Excuse me, Sir . . ."

"Send them in." Henry motioned.

Hector pushed Chief Warrant Officer Hendricks into the room, following closely behind. "Just pulling out of the drive," he explained.

"Why, Hendricks?" the Commander asked.

"Oldest reason in the book, Sir. Money! Oh! I have that report for the detective." He reached into his attache and pulled out a small revolver. Before anyone could react he put it to his head and pulled the trigger.

Four letter words and expressions of dismay filled the room. Hector shook his head in disbelief.

"I should have checked. I never saw it coming!" he said, "never saw it coming."

23

Saturday, October 5.
Adjustments

No one, by this time, was seated. "Obviously, we will not be continuing our meeting in the wake of this disastrous event," Henry noted soberly. "We still have a few things to discuss, and I'm curious as to why we're blessed with your appearance here, young lady," he said, nodding to Jennifer.

We all spilled out into the vestibule as the coroner pulled up to the front entry. There we split into small groups and chatted with our counterparts for a few minutes.

I walked to Lieutenant Commander Martaise and introduced myself. The commander, joined by Warrant Officer Fernando had an arm around Fox, both expressing their empathy at her ordeal. Hector, who was visibly shaken by the sudden appearance of a gun that the top policeman should have discovered and seized, was engaged in a somber discussion with Jennifer and Ensign Brady.

Henry came over to me. "Quite an afternoon, Garrett. Fourteen years, I believe, and threw it away for a few dollars! You've certainly stirred up a hornet's nest with your arrival, but I appreciate the house cleaning. I just hope the sweeping is done.

Listen," he continued, "let's do a reset early next week. Say Monday at 0900 hours. Include Hector. Does that sound good?"

"Not sure, Sir; any time is good for Liz and me, but I believe Jennifer has classes at that time. And Hector? Who knows."

Lieutenant Commander Martaise took a quick poll. Moments later we were all in agreement. The commander announced he'd cater a luncheon meeting 1100 hours at Coast Guard Headquarters Monday, October 7.

Henry pulled me aside as we were about to leave. "Here's that copy of the report you asked for." I glanced at the list of perhaps ten vessels. I'd study and follow up on them later. Henry continued.

"You have good instincts, Garrett. Ensign Brady tells me you think that young Jennifer may be a good candidate for a Harbor Master position. You and I know I can't just throw a college student in such an important position. But right now we have no one. I'm willing to listen to your ideas."

"Some sort of interim part-time duty to assist your own field officers," I shrugged, "possibly a practicum as part of her studies at Florida Keys Community. She's trying to decide between Criminology and a Fisheries Warden major or something similar. And she's not in a hurry to go to the big cities. Perfect candidate for a long-term commitment."

"Or not," Henry laughed.

"Or not," I agreed, laughing. "Incidently, Henry, I have a GPS tracker on the Brazilian yacht."

"Oh, you're a sly one, Garrett!"

As we hopped into the Mustang, Jennifer's phone rang. She stood with the door open as she answered. When she hung up, she poked her head in and looked at Liz.

"Do you have a boyfriend or relative that lives in the area?"

"I have no one except Gumshoe here. Why?"

"That was Dad. He says someone was nosing around Room 23, knocked, tried the door, peered in the windows . . . Dad went out, asked him if he needed help; the guy said 'no, he was just hoping to see his friend before he went back to Miami, that he might try again later'."

"Was the guy walking or driving?"

"Black sedan."

"Huh!" I said, nodding my head. "Our bus driver shooter, no doubt."

"That's what Dad thought, too. That's why he took the license plate number as the sedan left."

"Better get back before he gets himself in trouble," Liz suggested.

"I agree. Jump in Jen. Let's go."

"Could my dad be in danger?" she asked as she shut the door and buckled her seat belt.

"These guys play hardball, Jen," I cautioned,

"this one in particular. He won't stop until we stop him."

Five minutes later we were parked in front of the check-in. I went in while the two ladies walked around to our new unit--#41--strategically situated in the far corner (the motel was single story in an "L" shape).

"Mr. Little," I greeted the owner, "I'm Alan Garrett. Good to meet you."

"Likewise. Call me Bob. You and the lady are in Room 41, right? I've heard all about your adventures and the killings in the last week. How can I help you?"

"Just be a bit more cautious. Getting the license number of the black sedan was a brave thing to do, but . . ."

"I take down every license plate that registers here, Alan. An eighteen year habit," he said, handing me the plate number of the sedan.

"Did you give it to the police?"

"No, wanted your opinion first."

"Well, stay inside, Bob. If you see the black sedan call me, please. Liz and I are going to be checking out a few boats this afternoon, but we'll be close. Call Hector--bring him up to date on the fella and that sedan."

"Don't worry about me. I have a Glock 9mm and a 12 gauge behind the counter. All legal."

"Just be careful," I cautioned.

Fifteen minutes later Liz and I were heading for the first of twelve heavy working vessels, mostly tugs, but a couple of barges as well. All had moved the night of October one, the night *The Blue Moon* was dragged out two miles.

Fernando's staff had done a fine job putting this list together . . . they had two pages: page one was the list numbered one through twelve--page two was a map of the local marinas with the berth of each vessel number circled. *Piece of cake . . . should have it all done by the end of the day . . .* or so I thought.

It was just after 6:30 p.m. We had gone through seven of the boats and just about to step aboard number eight, a tug boat tied up north of Key West, when Jennifer called.

"Alan, come quick! Black sedan pulled up a few minutes ago. Three guys broke into Room 23. Dad called Hector, then called the room. Told the guys to get out of the room, that they had no right to go in... the guy on the phone just laughed and demanded to know where Liz had moved. Then one of them started out the door with a gun. Dad shot at him with his pistol . . . he thinks he wounded him. The guy went back in.

Hector is on his way; Dad's outside with a shotgun pointed at the door; Mom's with me inside our place, and we're scared! I have Dad's pistol, but I'm not sure I can use it.

All the units have patio doors that open to the pool area! There are probably five or six people sitting around out there right now. I'm scared for them, Gumshoe. Hurry!"

"Can you shoo them out of the pool area without attracting the wrong attention?" I asked. "Maybe bring them into the manager's suite until Hector is on-scene?"

"I'll try, but I'll be happy to see your Mustang."

24

Saturday, October 5.
Evening hours
Room 23

Hector pulled up in front of *The Chelsea House* a few minutes before Fox and I drove in, but we were both too late; the intruders from the sedan had slipped out through the patio door, overpowered three guests, two women and one youngster and herded them into Room 23. Jennifer gave me the news.

The pool area had been cleared, all patio doors locked and curtains drawn. The two units on either side of #23 were emptied. Now it was a matter of dealing with those inside. Hector took the lead. Three more squad cars rolled up, most of the Key West police force.

"You in the room!" Hector yelled. "This is Police Chief Hector Rodriguez. State your business!"

"You know our business!" the answer came back. "Give us the swimmer and the P.I. from California! Five minutes!"

"That will never happen, and you know it! Who am I talking to?"

"Your worst nightmare, Hector! I got a crew coming in a few minutes! We'll light up this town if you don't turn those two over. Four minutes and counting! I'm going to open the curtains so you can witness how serious I am, Mr. Hector Rodriguez!"

I walked over to Dave who was holding the shotgun. "Those windows in front--they're safety glass, right?"

"Yes, by code. Why?"

"Tempered or laminated?" I asked.

"Tempered, all tempered. What are you getting at, Alan?"

"I've got an idea . . . the element of surprise. Risky, but when you fight fire . . ."

"What's your surprise?"

"To save three people," I answered, "I'm going in through a window."

"Three minutes!" came the voice from within. The curtains didn't open.

I shared my plan with Hector. He nodded his head. Then I walked along the walkway from five or six units beyond #23 and edged back so I was standing directly in front of one of the two picture windows of the unit, praying that I had the right window, and waited.

"Two minutes!" came the voice, this time with urgency, almost despair.

"Maybe we can resolve this peacefully!" Hector called out. He prepared himself at the other window, but not quite so dramatically.

He had stationed a crew of four officers in the rear, and enough fire power to take out a small army. Two of those four were equipped with smoke bombs--and instructed to blow out the patio door glass and drop the canisters inside on his signal.

Only harsh laughter met Hector's olive branch. From inside came, "Time's up, Mr. Hector Rodriguez!"

The curtains opened. I stared, not even ten inches from a garish grin. Glass exploded. My first shot went through his forehead. His smile was gone along with half his head.

The hostage screamed. Thousands of tempered glass shards exploded around me as I stepped through the window over the would-be killer and his butcher knife.

In the confusion I caught another of the kidnappers in the butt with two quick taps from my .45. He would live, but he might walk funny for awhile.

While I was causing my own planned confusion, the police were doing the same on the other windows. Hector shattered and walked through that window, while one of the four officers in the rear, trying to breach the unit was shot in the elbow by the third henchmen. Hector caught that thug with two shots through the stomach and chest.

As it quieted down, none of the hostages were injured in the melee. The only injury was to Room 23. None of the 'so-called crew' promised ever arrived.

After fifteen minutes, Hector disbursed his squad cars to their regular tasks; one of the units shuttled the wounded would-be killer to the hospital. Hopefully, he would provide us with useful information. The chief stayed behind with the coroner to wrap up the chaotic scene. Two villains were deceased. They took a ride to the police morgue. None of the three carried any identification.

Several motel guests gathered in the pool area to console the three rescued guests that joined them. Life slowly returned to 'almost' normal at *The Chelsea House.*

* * *

It was getting late; Dave and Jennifer assessed the damages to their room. I followed them inside.

"Whatever costs the insurance won't cover, let me know," I told them, "I'll take care of them."

"You will do no such thing!" Dave shot back. "Between the insurance and city I should be well reimbursed for any losses. Besides I haven't been in the middle of such excitement since I played in the state championship basketball game in 1973."

"Okay," I agreed; "then let me do this, because none of this would have happened, had Liz and I not been staying here . . . let me cater a full buffet breakfast for you and all the guests tomorrow morning around the pool."

"I can't let you d . . ."

"Yes, you can, Dave. My treat! I need only the number of guests staying here tonight, I'll do the rest."

After more grumbling, we retreated to our separate quarters, and a few minutes later Jennifer called with the number: fifty-one guests. Ten minutes later I made a catering company very happy.

25

Sunday, October 6.
Sweet and Sour

The Sunday morning breakfast was a hit for everyone that could make it. The caterers set up tables and by 7 a.m. had pancakes on the griddle, bacon and eggs with hash browns, bowls of fruit and cold cereal. Coffee and juice was always available in the lobby, but Dave and his wife went from table to table refilling mugs and glasses.

At 7:20 we saw smoke far to the north of us, and a couple of engines and a police unit from Key West headed north on Highway One. Fires like this were usually boats, and usually handled by Fire Hose boats, but it was worrying.

The conversations here were upbeat; last night's ordeal became old history. Even those held hostage were bright and cheery. The caterers policed the area to perfection and disappeared at 10 a.m. Success all around.

Dave and his wife came over to Fox and me and gave us a hug.

"That went so well, Alan, we just might do this once or twice every year as a thank you to our guests for choosing *The Chelsea House*," Dave said, smiling broadly.

Fox and I then returned to our yesterday's task of verifying where the heavy vessels were the night of October 1. We had gone through seven, and were just preparing to board the eighth last evening when we received that distress call from Jennifer.

We wanted to finish this task as quickly as possible today, then we were going to the hospital to question the culprit from last night . . . the one still alive. So, five boats to go.

Eighth on the Coast Guard list was one of three vessels working out of docks north of Key West. This one was a seagoing, deep-sea tug, larger and stronger than a smaller, harbor type.

"Permission to come aboard," I yelled at the first sailor I saw.

"For what purpo . . . oh! Yur that P.I. couple down here lookin' fer some kid, ain'tcha? An' you wanna know where we was workin' las' Tuesday night. Am I right? Shore. Come on aboard."

I looked at Fox, frowning . . . *lookin' for some kid?* How did he know that? Fox returned my quizzical look with one of her own.

Our guide led us to the Captain's quarters. A lanky, bespectacled fellow looked up at us from his swiveled armchair. He looked to be in his late 60's, maybe 70. His unkempt shoulder-length reddish brown hair belied the voice and vocabulary of education. I sized him up to be a 1970's moneyed Berkeley brat who tossed a coin . . . would it be the Oregon "back to the earth" crowd or the Everglades. *The Mother Earth News* lost out to the Alligators.

Across from him was another obviously distraught mariner of about 40. Each had a half-filled glass and there was a bottle on the table. Our host introduced himself as Captain Jakes, his friend, Captain Turner. Liz and I did the same.

"We heard you were looking at all of us deep water rigs. We were expecting you yesterday, but heard you had an emergency you needed to attend.

Come, sit, have a drink!" Jakes invited. "To answer your question, *No*, I didn't pull *The Blue Moon* out to sea, but Turner, here, did."

I pulled a chair back for Fox and sat across from her, reached for the bottle and poured two six ounce glasses to the half, then topped our two new friends' glasses to an equal amount.

"We're listening," I said, taking a sip, and pushing my fedora further back.

Turner began, "Dead. They're all friggin' dead! All my men! My boat! All gone! Explosion, just this morning."

"Who, Turner! Who?" Liz asked.

"They paid me $20,000 to drag her out. Told me it was a movie scene. I was going to get another $30K to bring her back in after the scene was finished. Hell, who doesn't want an easy $50K for measly twelve hours' work?"

Seeing that his friend was too shook up to continue, Jakes broke in.

"His boat was torched shortly after 7 a.m. this morning. You may have seen the smoke. His crew had just finished a job, pulling a yacht off a reef up at Big Coppitt Key. Got back in around 3 a.m.

Three of the crew, single fellows, bunked in the boat. They didn't have a chance. Turner and two others went home."

Turner continued, "Three of the finest men you could ever work with or call friends. Gone! The sons'a'bitches!"

"Can you tell us who, Turner?" I asked.

"No. Just a phone call last Monday for the agreement, and then about noon on Tuesday, a kid on a bike with a big envelope filled with cash."

"Two questions. Was it sealed?" I asked. "Do you still have the envelope?"

"Yes, it was sealed . . . and no, I tossed it after I pulled the cash out."

"On the boat?"

"No. Why?"

Jakes answered. "Finger prints or DNA from saliva if it was licked, Turner."

"Ahhh, let me think. I, uhh, I counted all the money while I was sitting in my truck, stuffed the money in my pocket, made sure the envelope was empty, folded it up I remember, and, uh, yeah, I remember! I dumped it in the trash can at the Chevron station."

"We'll go look for it, Mr. Garrett," Jakes assured me. "Let's hope it's still there. If so, we'll bring it to you. I'll let you know."

I took one last sip before I stood. "One thing we've learned today. Evil is still at work in the Keys! Can we do anything for you in regard to your loss?" I continued.

"Naw," Turner said, regaining his composure. "Insurance will cover most of it I expect. We all have insurance--boat as well. Workin' the water you got to. Agent has been and gone already. Boat's a total write-off, but I got all the papers at the house.

Just gotta bury my boys. They didn't have no family that I know of."

Liz gave them each one of her cards. "Let us know if we can help," she said, taking my arm. We said our goodbyes and started down the ramp when a question popped up. I turned.

"There had to be another vessel out there, Turner," I began. "Maybe a fish boat, a yacht, something? You just towed *The Blue Moon* out there . . . wasn't there another boat out on the water?"

"Yeah, there was, come to think of it; a zodiac with cameraman aboard, shooting the movie scene. Didn't think much more about it. He was yelling, 'make sure you bring the kid!'"

"Thanks. Are you certain he said, *'make sure you bring the kid'*?

"Yes. Definitely! High, shrill voice . . . now that I think of it, could have been a gal. Probably a guy, though."

"You say a Medline type. Not familiar with it but I'll look it up. Might not be anything, but might be very important. Thanks again--and take care."

26

Sunday, October 6.
Touching base with Hector

When we left Captains Jakes and Turner, we were lost in thought and hardly spoke as we returned to our motel unit. Fox went immediately to her computer to check the location of the Brazilian yacht while I poured Martell for each of us.

Fox sat on her bed, I sat at the table– nothing fancy, simply motel water glasses. "She hasn't moved. Still in Havana . . . at least the GPS is still there," she laughed.

I frowned and changed the subject. "Liz, check the different zodiacs, print off a few pictures of the Medline type. We'll bring it up tomorrow at the meeting with the Coast Guard."

"Sure, Bossman. What do you think of Captain Turner's statement? You know, recalling the guy on the zodiac yelling, *'make sure you bring the kid'*!"

"Or a gal," I reminded her. "Remember he said it could have been a gal. Two things for sure, Fox, Paul was alive and on *The Blue Moon* when you were on it, and while aboard he was probably being held prisoner just as you were."

I called General Maggorie to bring him up to date; his only remark was a groan, and a verbal expletive. He was definitely unhappy with our lack of progress. I must admit, I felt like chasing after the yacht and boarding her immediately, but she was now in Cuban waters; our Coast Guard was useless.

"I'm hungry, Bossman. Let's have dinner."

"Good idea. *The Hungry Pelican?*" I grabbed my fedora and reached for the door. At the same time a sharp rap at the door startled me. I jerked my hand back and reached for my .45.

"Alan. You in there?" It was Hector.

"We are," Liz called out as I opened the door and re-holstered my .45.

"We were just on our way to dinner," Fox said. "Interested in joining us?"

"No. No time. Just wanted you to know the fellow you shot at the motel yesterday is out of the hospital and in the jail. That's the good news. The bad news is that the FBI called me this morning after the tug boat fire that killed three; you heard about that, right?"

"Yes, we heard. So just what is the FBI going to do?" I asked.

"With all the deaths, your shootings, Coast Guard suicide and such, they're taking a lead role. They'll be in my office at 3 p.m. tomorrow afternoon, and I'd like you there."

"That's fine. Are you still planning to be at our luncheon at the Coast Guard facility tomorrow morning?"

"Yes. I'll be there."

"Good. Look forward to it. With all that we've heard about the FBI involvement in unethical procedures, I'm not so sure I want them here . . . but they are, theoretically, the top domestic law enforcement agency in the country. Maybe I shouldn't be so judgmental."

"I'll be off," Hector said. "Enjoy your dinner. See you tomorrow morning."

We enjoyed Atlantic salmon with zucchini and Caesar salad.

*   *   *

We spent the rest of the evening calling friends back in California. I started with Pop.

27

Monday, October 7.
Lunch with The Coast Guard

We were all there: Commander Henry Waite, Hector, Lieutenant Commander Martaise, Ensign Brady, Jennifer Little, Warrant Officer Fernando, Fox and me . . . and one more.

JAG attorney, Sandra Eliot, whom I knew very well. She and I--when I was with AFOSI--had worked in league on several legal matters; definitely a competent lawyer. I could only surmise the Commander had asked her to fly down should there be any repercussions surrounding Hendricks' suicide. She sat at my right side for the luncheon. Fox seemed a bit nettled sitting across from me.

The caterers were top notch, putting my motel spread to shame . . . of course, they had the budget of the federal government behind them.

The discussion around the table turned to the important points of current events. We started with Hendricks, an unmarried officer. His house had been scoured from one end to the other; his bank accounts and files were being examined as we were enjoying lunch. The investigating team called Henry with news: they had found evidence linking Hendricks with Harbor Master Buck Watters.

Hector spoke, "Speaking of Watters, we found a cache of drugs with a street value close to a half million USD in his cottage, along with a computer and a bag of thumb drives. My men are going through them as time permits. So far, we've found only videos of scantily clad young ladies on yachts and some porn. There's an Excel program set up but nothing in the columns. The only thing on the page is a series of letters and numbers in the heading."

"I'd like a copy of that Excel file," Sandra Eliot smiled up at Hector, "and access to the computer if you don't mind."

"Of course, Ma'am," he said. "The FBI requested access as well. They're meeting us at 3 p.m. in my office. Join us."

Everyone around the table looked up at the news of the FBI's interest in Key West. Sandra Eliot especially so.

"Wow, that's a surprise!" she said, looking at me, then Henry. "I shall."

"What's next on our agenda?" Henry asked.

Sandra Eliot stood. "I'd like to know what my old friend, Alan Garrett is doing in Key West. State your business, please, Mr. Garrett."

"I suppose I haven't shared everything I'm doing down here," I began. Fox cleared her throat and rolled her eyes. "*We* are doing down here," I corrected myself. Everyone laughed.

"Fox and I are here in search of a young man, who, in a spirit and act of rebellion, defied his father, stole classified information, and came to Florida . . . where he was kidnapped. We," I said, nodding to Fox, "believe him to be on the Brazilian yacht, *Bordereau,* which was last known to be in Havana."

"Why was the yacht not boarded and searched while here?" Ms. Eliot asked.

"Good question, Ma'am," I smiled, "but I cannot ask it of those assigned to that task . . . they're both dead."

"Huh! Another question, Mr. Garrett, "why do you think she's in Havana?"

"I put a GPS signal on one of her sailors."

"Okay," Henry said, "anything else to report? We had a tugboat burn up yesterday morning. Three lives lost; I already know that tug was on the list we provided to you, Alan. I already know you talked to the pilot, Captain Tucker . . . hell, you even talked to him before we did! How?"

"Just going down the list, Sir. He was with his buddy, Jakes. We visited the Jakes' tug first."

"Learn anything?" Henry asked.

"Two or three things, Sir," Fox spoke up. "Tucker was contracted to pull *The Blue Moon* out."

She went through the agreement, the kid on the bike, the manila envelope, the other details . . . when she got to the Medline Zodiac she pulled pictures from her purse and passed them around. "Captain Tucker said the person on the zodiac yelled, *'make sure you bring the kid'!* so we now know Paul was alive and on that old derelict, and we know the kidnappers were on the zodiac. You need to find that zodiac."

"There are at least a dozen Medlines running around these waters," Henry put his hands in the air in exasperation, "and more coming in all the time. How do we find the right one?"

"You hire a private investigator," Fox answered to the delight of all those present. Even I had to smile. "All craft, beginning in the early 1970's are required to have a Hull Identification Number, or HIN, right? It's a simple matter of charting those based in the Keys."

"We'll take care of it, Ma'am," Henry assured her.

Fox couldn't let it go. "By the way, if you need a frogman let me know," she said raising an eyebrow, while grinning at the commander.

"So," the commander looked around the table for affirmation, "we're going to chart every Medline in the area. Can their movements of the last week be verified? No. But we can ask nicely." Turning to Ensign Brady, the Commander simply said, "Ensign." She replied, "Yes, Sir."

"What's next?" the Commander asked.

"The matter of replacing the Harbor Master, Sir," Lieutenant Commander Martaise reminded him.

"Yes, and not only the Harbor Master," Henry said, "but the assistant as well. We all know the Harbor Master is a civilian position under the auspices of this office, so for the time being, I'm assigning one of our own to fill the vacancy.

In addition, we have a young lady here today who expresses a desire to explore taking on the role once she has some training." Henry motioned for Jennifer to stand. She complied, and waved nervously to the group. Henry said, "Meet Jennifer Little." All eyes were upon her. "Tell us a bit about yourself."

I had to hand it to Henry for putting her on the spot. But even more, I was proud of Jen for remaining calm.

"Well!" she looked around, "I wasn't expecting to be put in a spotlight, but here I am. I'm twenty-one, going to Keys Community, and just this morning switched majors from Fisheries to Criminology as a first step in building a resume in law enforcement. I feel really fired up, thanks to Mr. Garrett and Ms. Fox."

Sandra Eliot broke in, "So this is an emotional decision based upon one weekend of excitement?"

"No, Ma'am. I love the Keys. I was born and raised here. I decided when I graduated from high school and entered Keys Community College I would make a difference in the local region. I thought, initially, Fisheries would be a good start, but in rethinking it, a better fit for me would be the port of entry."

"Do you have time in your schedule to work with one of our officers on a volunteer interim basis—let's say, eight to twelve hours weekly for three months?" Henry asked.

"Yes, Sir, so long as the officer can work with my schooling and motel duties."

The Commissioner turned to Ensign Brady once again, "Get the young lady's schedule, please. We'll put together a chart that will work for her."

Turning to Jennifer, Henry asked her to stay behind for a few minutes, and me the same.

"In the meantime gentlemen, ladies," Henry said, "I have great news. In the first few days of October our crews have confiscated more than $143 million in cocaine off our coasts in a series of sweeps. The drugs are being transported to Miami tomorrow morning on one of our cutters for disposal.

We're supposed to receive one of those new Legend-class cutters in the near future. Perhaps this bust will expedite delivery for us down here in Florida. Most of the the water drug busts have been made in the Pacific, but a Legend-class cutter will absolutely strengthen our arsenal. There is one now in the Carolinas; we've been assigned one, but we're not holding our breath."

"Good job on the seizure!" I said, raising a glass. Everyone around the table joined me.

After more casual conversation the meeting adjourned. Jennifer, Fox and I stayed behind per Henry's request.

"You mentioned you saw several more sailors board the Brazilian yacht than reported by Chief Warrant Officer Hendricks and Buck Watters. In your opinion, any of them U.S. citizens?"

"I see where you're going," I said, nodding my head. "Yes, one or two at least. That means you can board her anywhere on the the water, right?"

"That's correct."

"I would have said yes in any event, but I'm sure of it, Henry."

"Perhaps I can join you in your meeting this afternoon...?"

"I'm sure you'd be welcome. What are you planning?"

"Board the damn boat. We have two cutters in the Bahamas right now providing assistance following Hurricane Dorian's devastation. One of them is a medium endurance cutter with about a hundred crew; ought to be enough to scour that Brazilian yacht from one end to the other. If she's doing anything illegal we'll escort her back here. I'll need your GPS monitoring device, Garrett."

"No problem, I said, "I'll bring my computer to the meeting."

28

Monday, October 7.
Afternoon with The FBI

Fox and I were the first to arrive, followed by Sandra Eliot. We sat with Hector having a coffee when the FBI contingent arrived. There were three of them--two women, one man. Mid-thirties, sharp dressers all. It was 3 p.m. on the dot.

After introductions one of the ladies came right to the point. "Mr. Garrett, I understand you are here in search of a young teenager. What's his name?"

Henry Ware poked his head into the room about that time. "Sorry I'm late," he apologized, seating himself beside Hector. Then he poured himself a cup of coffee and sat back, listening.

The interruption was only momentary; I had already formulated my answer.

"No offence, Ma'am. Client has asked me to keep that information confidential," I replied. My answer took her aback.

"Mr. Garrett! This is the FBI you're talking to, not some podunk backwoods sheriff from Mayberry, RFD. Who is your client?" her voice raised a few decibels.

"Understood, Ma'am. My answer is the same. I don't want any embarrassment for this office, the FBI or anyone involved here today. I'm here on a private matter; I'd like to keep it that way. If you wish," I scribbled a phone number on a note pad and handed it to her, "here's a private number to call."

She took the note with a "pshhh" sound . . . then looked at the number. The area code was 212. She called the number--calling my bluff.

"Who is this?" she asked briskly. Then, "Yes, Sir. . . . this is FBI senior agent Teresa Hughes. I'm calling regarding a certain Alan Garrett who says his business is private and confidential. He's being rather belligerent, and I . . . yes, Sir. I understand, Sir. Thank you, Sir . . . yes, Sir."

There was a noticeable period of silence. She handed me the phone. "The Attorney General would like to speak with you."

After a quick chat I handed the phone back to Ms. Hughes.

"We're done here," she said, her face twitching. "We may nose around a bit, but only in a supportive effort. Good day, good luck, ladies, gentlemen." They were gone.

"What the hell just happened?" Hector asked. "I thought they were going to stick around and annoy us for days. You have some clout, Mister!"

"Sometimes it's not what you know . . ." I offered, shrugging.

That triggered an explosion from Sandra Eliot.

"Bullshit! There's not a political bone in your body, Alan Garrett! Everything you've earned you've earned with merit. Don't you dare put your investigative skills down!"

"My hero!" Fox giggled snaking an arm through mine and pulling me toward her.

"Stop it!" I said, smiling. "Back to business. I think our problem in the Keys with the tug tragedy means the bad guys continue to tie up loose ends--one of which is you," I said, turning to Fox. "They won't stop until we stop them."

"What are you going to do about the kid?" Sandra wanted to know.

"We think we know where he is--on board a Brazilian yacht. Arrangements are being made right now to bring him here within two or three days."

I gave Henry my computer with instructions for access to the GPS monitor. He nodded.

"Maybe it's a good thing for a JAG attorney to be in Key West," Sandra smiled.

"I think we have it handled, Ma'am," Henry winked at her, "but I'm glad you're with us nonetheless."

* * *

Hector closed the meeting by opening the refrigerator and bringing out a wrapped platter of small, open sandwiches, cubes of cheese varieties and a bottle of Lillet Blanc.

"Ahh," I laughed, "I was hoping we could go to the dungeon and visit a couple of inmates, but that can wait a half hour or so. Lillet (Lee-Lay) was the aperitif of choice for James Bond. Where's the slice of orange?"

Hector was quick to apologize. "My maid has the day off. Where are my manners?" He reached into the freezer, pulled out a bowl filled with frozen orange slices, ice cubes and tongs. "You're on your own," he said, "but only one drink each, otherwise you'll be arrested."

I grabbed a whiskey sour glass and the tongs, poured the liquid over two cubes of ice and a slice of orange. The others followed suit. Hector reached for a sandwich.

* * *

It was after 4:30 p.m. when we entered the jail. We visited Kate's cell first. She was still sticking to her story; she was to ignore completely or make only cursory boardings on certain vessels as they entered the harbor.

Her instructions came from brief phone calls, a man, always a different burner phone; sizeable cash deposits were then made into an offshore account in her name.

"You need a signature to open an account," Sandra said. "How did you manage that?"

"Within the first week of my being installed as associate Harbor Master I received an anonymous phone call. The voice said, check your mail box, then hung up. When I checked there was a form to fill out with instructions to put it back in the mailbox. I did. When I next looked the envelope was gone."

"And you didn't think something was wrong with that picture?" Fox asked.

Kate stared at Fox for a couple of seconds. "It was you I almost killed, wasn't it?"

"Yes, as a matter of fact it was. But here I am."

"I'm so sorry," Kate whimpered. "I was offered $300,000. I refused. He offered me $500,000 as a final offer, then said he would have it done by someone hungrier, and both you and I would be eliminated. I was scared out of my wits, still am. These people are dangerous!"

"You're the only female in the holding cell." Hector assured her. "We have only one other prisoner, and he's cuffed in a bunk in the men's section."

"Tell me, Kate, where is your little cache of loot?" Henry asked.

"Still in Belize," Hector supplied.

We couldn't have orchestrated it better . . . "Belize?" Fox and I blurted out together. "Where in Belize?" I asked.

"The Atlantic International Bank in Belize City," Hector answered. "You've no doubt heard of it."

"Yes, yes . . . I just came from there not ten days ago on another job. The country is a corporate tax haven . . . I'm wondering why they set her up there?"

"We, that is, the FBI has frozen the account," Hector continued, "with just short of $1.3 million in it."

"I've never even looked at the account to check," Kate stammered. "Over a million dollars?"

"Do we know where the deposits come from?" I asked.

"All done under the radar, I'm sure," Sandra said.

"I may be able to help with that," I frowned. "I'm not sure, but I made a friend or two while I was there."

"Tell me, Ms. Moore, how much of the Belize account funding have you withdrawn?" Henry asked.

"None, as I said," Kate replied, visibly shaking. "Everything I've done is out of fear for my life. I should have come to you, Chief Rodriguez, but I was afraid for you as well.

I was told they would send in a terrorist cell and destroy the entire police force, bomb the hospital and set Key West back a hundred years."

By now, Kate was crying. When she regained her composure she added, "I think I need an attorney."

"While you're mulling that over," Hector said, "we'll have a talk with our wounded tenant." He led us past the gate and into the men's section of the jail. The prisoner was sitting in the first cell, reading a Spanish newspaper. He was dressed in a tee-shirt and shorts.

Fox spoke only English, in fact the only person in the cell block who didn't speak Spanish; she stood and listened to the entire conversation without butting in.

Hector called out, "Adolfo! Company!"

"Do you have my dinner?" the young man demanded. "I haven't eaten since early this morning. You should feed the people you hold. You shoot me, put me in jail, I can't get out on bail, and then you starve me. I will make a formal complaint!"

"Who is your boss?" I asked.

"I spit on you!" was the reply I got.

Next was Sandra. "If you'd like any kind of *nice* treatment, Adolfo, please know we need some cooperation from you."

"I spit on all of you!" he screamed. "The boss will destroy Key West and all of you! We have forces just waiting for him to give the signal."

Hector laughed at the outburst, "You lost all rights when you became a terrorist, Adolfo, but I tell you what. I'll call up right now to see when your dinner will be coming.

Any of you folks want to join us? Henry? Ms. Eliot? I need a head count. I'll cater the dinner from the place Henry used this morning. How about you two, Garrett?"

All of us declined the invitation. He dialed a number.

"No," I answered, "I think we' ll head back to the motel. Do you have a minute, Henry?"

Before he could answer, Hector butted in, "A catered dinner for us in the jail will be coming within a half hour. I'll be joining you, Adolfo. We'll have dinner together. Maybe even a bottle of wine."

Nothing more was to be gained by questioning Adolfo; he was belligerent and filled with hatred.

The group dissolved at this point. Fox and I said our goodbyes and walked outside. Henry followed. We discussed with some laughter, some questions and some shaking of heads the differences between the two incarcerated.

Then the discussion turned to my missing teen. "Have you heard anything from your cruiser?" I asked.

"Nothing yet," Henry said, "but I'll keep you on speed dial," he laughed.

Fox and I drove back to the motel. We parked my mustang and walked down to the marina.

"Beautiful evening, Gumshoe. I could live in Florida. You?"

"No. Dorian went through here in September, remember? Missed Key West by a whisker, damn near destroyed the Bahamas . . . and that was before terrorists invaded this fair city. I'll stick with the devil I know." We were unaware that a different kind of evil was coming . . . and not an act of God. Impending disaster was coming upon the fair community of Key West.

29

Tuesday, October 8.
Shortly after midnight

The explosion rattled every window in the motel room. As I threw my pants on I looked at the digital clock on the night stand. Big red letters told me it was 1:22 a.m. Instinctively I grabbed my .45. Fox was just emerging from her room wrapped in a robe.

"What was that, Bossman? Sounded like dynamite just outside our windows."

The answer came in the form of another blast, this one further away. My cellphone rang, then the room phone. I had an unsettling feeling in my stomach as I grabbed my cell.

"Mr. Garrett! You awake?"

"I am now. Who's this?"

"Officer Timothy White. You remember me, right?"

"I do." I said, as another blast shook the windows . . . "any idea what's going on?"

"Explosion at the police station. It's on fire. I'm standing right in front of it. There's not much left. Don't know about the other two blasts."

"Why are you calling me, Tim? Where's Hector?"

Liz hung up the motel phone. "That was Jennifer," she whispered. "She's worried."

"I don't know, Sir. Hector doesn't pick up." Tim was saying. "I thought, *'who can I call?'* I still had your business card in my wallet, so I called you."

"I'm flattered, Tim. I'll be right there," I said, and ended the call.

"I'm going with you. Give me a second, just need to throw some clothes on."

"What's Jennifer worried about?" I asked as we hopped into the mustang.

"She says just a bad feeling."

"That makes two of us," I said.

"Three," came her reply.

The short drive took under four minutes. The police headquarters was ablaze with two fire units drenching it with water. Tim White met us out on the street, watching, along with four or five other officers, and a few townfolk.

"Anybody inside?" I asked.

"Five," Tim said. "Desk sergeant, Mike Broderick, the two jailers and both prisoners. No survivors."

"And Hector?" Fox asked.

"He's at the main marina. Coast Guard cutter was destroyed by another blast. He lives very near there. He called just after you and I hung up."

"So, he's okay. Good. Sorry about the others. Do you know anything about the third blast, Tim?"

"Two of our guys rolled on it. West end of town, toward the Coast Guard Headquarters."

"Have they called you back?" I asked.

Tim turned to his fellow officers. "Anybody hear from Mateo or Rubin?"

The answer was yes. Rubin reported that terrorists had set a charge meant to destroy the Coast Guard Headquarters, but the blast caused only slight damage to a small section of the venerable, old building. A very unskilled attempt.

The police chief's car squealed to a stop behind one of the fire engines. Hector stepped out.

"Did we lose any more?" he asked.

"No, sir. Just the five we told you about," one of the officers said.

"Why is the private eye here?" then turning to me he asked, "why are you here, Garrett?"

"Courtesy call," I started.

"I called him, Sir," Tim White interrupted. "I couldn't reach you so I called him."

"What about Captain Thune?" Hector looked around, sounding frustrated. "Where the hell is he anyway?"

"The captain is on vacation until October 28, but we're trying to track him down, Sir."

"When did Thune leave?" I asked, frowning. "I saw him at *the Hungry Pelican* just Friday morning."

Hector gave me a sidelong look of *"hey Garrett! This is my city, my questions . . . back off."*

As he glared at me, Tim White answered his question.

"He left just yesterday morning. He had three weeks coming. He and his wife were to drive up to

Miami, then scheduled to fly out to Gatwick last night. We'll find them."

"No. Let them enjoy their time away. Let's find the scum that attacked our town. Is the FBI team still here? Let's bring them in on this. What was the gal's name . . . Teresa Hughes? I had her card, but it was probably destroyed in the blast. Firemen won't let us in there yet.

Garrett, I think it best for you and Fox to leave Key West. I can't force you, but it seems our troubles started with your lady's arrival."

"You couldn't be more wrong, Sir. We simply uncovered some rot plaguing your town. On the other hand, I agree . . . this isn't our fight. Our search for the lad will continue as soon as I have a seaworthy craft--a day, perhaps two."

"Fair enough, Garrett," Hector held out his hand. "Fair enough."

I shook his hand. "Sorry we couldn't be of more help. Fox let's go back to the motel."

It was 4 a.m. "Breakfast at 6?" Liz agreed. I took a quick shower, donned a robe and fell across the bed. I didn't sleep.

30

Wednesday, October 9.
Breakfast and Boat Hunting

It was 5:50 a.m. We stopped just long enough at the motel office to let Jennifer know we wouldn't be staying much longer, nor would she and I have our morning run.

"I'm so sorry you're leaving us," she said, "but I knew it had to end soon.

"I'll be looking for a seaworthy boat to charter, then we're gone," I told her. "Have a good boat for us?" I laughed.

"No, but you've met Sam and Ernie at *the Hungry Pelican* haven't you?" Jennifer asked. Then she laughed. "They know every boat for sale at most of the local marinas, including the prices, the bargains, which ones to stay away from, the whole ball of wax. Two walking boat experts."

"We're on our way there for breakfast right now, but they won't be there this early I'm sure," I said. "Fox and l will take a stroll on a few marinas before lunch. Maybe we can check in with those two experts over lunch."

Surprisingly, the place was bustling, including a table in the center that seated ten. Seven old-timers were already gathered around it, hands wrapped around steaming mugs of coffee.

"Morning, Alan! Morning, Fox!" Marge sang out. "Pick a spot and park yourselves; I'll be with you in a minute with coffee."

"Hey!" one of the old-timers yelled, "you're the two California detectives ain't you?" He pulled a chair out and motioned, "Sit here with us. We heard the police station got blowed up last night. What can you tell us about that?"

Fox and I joined them; we sat across from each other and said our "howdys" to the group. I pushed my fedora further back so I could read the menu.

Marge brought the coffee and took our orders. I answered a few of their questions--as I knew them--about the early morning terrorism, then it was my turn to ask a question.

"I'm looking for a boat to rent or charter. Has to be fast, has to be rigged out with sleeper, galley and shower. Anybody here know of such a boat that might be available?"

One old fellow said, "Plenty of boats just sitting at the marinas around here, should be somethin' would fit your needs. Wanna do a coupla day's fishing?"

Marge refilled our coffee mugs and brought our orders while he was asking the question.

"No," I answered, "I'm thinking, perhaps charter one for five to ten days, seaworthy enough for trips to the Bahamas or Dominican Republic, that kind of thing."

"Oh! Doin' a mite of drug runnin' are ya?" the fellow sitting next to Fox laughed, patting her on the shoulder.

"Why not?" Fox shot back. "Nothing like a bit of adventure."

"No, all legal, I can assure you," I smiled.

Looking around our new friend continued, "Where's Ernie? He and Sam were supposed to be here. Ernie would point you to the right boat."

Around the table heads nodded in agreement. Fox looked at me, shrugging her shoulders.

I pushed my plate back and enjoyed the last few swallows from my mug. "Gentlemen, we'll be leaving you. When Sam and Ernie show up, tell them we'll be back here at noon."

"Here," Fox said to the fellow next to her, "my card, Mr. —?"

"Lenny, Ma'am."

"Have one of them call us."

Lenny studied the card for a moment. "Gumshoe and Fox? What's Gumshoe?" he asked.

"That's an old-fashioned name for a private eye," another old white-haired gent said. "Gimme one of them cards."

One by one they each asked for a card. Fox laughed and left a small stack on the table while I swiped my credit card for Marge.

"Where shall we start, Bossman?" Fox asked as we walked outside to the first streaks of morning light.

"How about the main marina?"

"The one where the yacht, *Bordereau,* was docked?" she asked.

"Sure, why not?"

Very often novice boat enthusiasts shell out thousands of dollars for a new beauty, lease a slip, take their new dream boat out for her maiden voyage, maybe even a second run.

Then, for a variety of reasons, disillusionment sets in; the boat floats--rocking idly in the slip until finally, neglected, it ends up with a phone number scrawled on a **For Sale** sign on the windshield. . . . Today we were looking at signs.

We walked the lengths of four pier fingers, Fox jotting phone numbers of possibles in her notebook, when someone shouted, "Hey, Gumshoe!" followed by laughter.

We looked up to see Ernie and Sam coming our way.

"Heard you was lookin' fer a boat, Gumshoe," Sam said with a chortle. "You know your way around boats?"

"Definitely," I answered, "but I'm not looking for a pleasure boat, fellas; I'm looking for a small, fast, working boat, similar to a cutter."

"You buyin' or rentin'?"

Fox interrupted, "Depends upon the price."

"Find anything?" Ernie asked

I showed them what we had found so far. He frowned as he read our list.

"Nah, none of them. I have just the boat for you. It's down at the marina close to your motel. C'mon, we'll meet you there."

"Whoa, fellas. We're still looking here," Fox protested. "Give us a break."

"Please yourself," Ernie said, "but you're just wasting your time."

"Okay, Ernie," I smiled, "we'll follow you there and look at this crackerjack of a boat. It can't hurt, and we have time."

* * *

It was as they said . . . perfect. A replica of an older coast guard cutter but much faster and more powerful, custom built in 2000 for a wealthy client who, after making a sizeable deposit, was killed in an auto accident. The builder sold it the same year for a song. It even had two M-240 machine guns mounted mid-ship on either side near the stern.

There was a catch—the boat belonged to Ernie—sly old fox; wherever the boat went, he went. To top it off, wherever Ernie went, Sam went.

"How much?" I asked.

"A hundred a day plus diesel, full tanks both ends of the trip. If the guns are in play, add another hundred."

"That's reasonable," I said.

"Plus an extra fifty fer me, an' supplies fer all of us, including booze."

"Just beer, no other booze," I corrected.

"When do you want to get underway?" Ernie asked.

"Tomorrow morning. Breakfast at the Pelican, say, 6:30. Then go," I decided.

"You make sure she's fueled, Fox will organize the food, I have a couple of errands to run. See you tomorrow morning."

* * *

I called Henry to make sure he was there. I was preparing to retrieve my computer and tracking bug. He surprised me.

"Just going to call you, Alan. My crew is about to board the *Bordereau.* I have live feed through skype. Come and watch with me."

I was there in minutes. Ensign Brady ushered me into Henry's office where a circle of officers was gathered around a large screen, audio crackling through the speakers. I joined the group.

"Commander," a female voice was saying, "we have a total of nineteen aboard. Eight have Brazilian passports, two Saudi, two Austrian . . . including Captain Bosignion, two have papers they call Cuban traveling documents and five with no passports. Three of them claim to be a team of U.S. Government scientists, working on a project for the CIA."

"What kind of project?" Henry asked her.

"Wouldn't say, Sir. Top secret."

"Any IDs."

"No documents of any kind."

I piped up, "Ask them if they have decoded the list and sent it to the AFOSI yet, and if not, why not?"

Henry looked at me quizzically, but went along with it.

"Did you hear the question, Captain?"

"Yes, Sir."

"Did you understand it?"

"Understood, Sir."

We tried to hear the conversation between the officer and the others, but we could make out only parts of it. The rest was unintelligible. The officer came back to us.

"Sir, they're still working on it. They think they've broken the code and will have it completed tomorrow morning."

"Ma'am, this is Alan Garrett, AFOSI out of DC. I'll be joining you tomorrow before 10 a.m. Tell the project leader to hand over the entire project to you, including their computers and any notes they may have. Then, before you hang up from the commander, you and I should have a private conversation. Thanks."

Henry ended the conversation abruptly. "Maintain your present coordinates, Captain. I may join Garrett tomorrow morning. He has something more to say. Take the phone off speaker. Here he is once again."

"Ma'am, I'm sure you're aware the project group is bogus as are probably the others on board. Please send Commander Waite mug shots and fingerprints of all on board. He'll run them using ABIS (Automated Biometric Identification System). Keep them shackled. No outside contact. We'll see you tomorrow morning."

31

Thursday, October 10.
Underway

No introductions were needed. Henry knew Sam and Ernie very well. He had even boarded Ernie's vessel, *My Second Choice*, a few years before and checked out the legitimacy of, and licensing permits for the guns and gun mounts. *All legal* he had said to Ernie's smile and Sam's laughter. Today would be a good day. Henry looked forward to it.

The boat was fast, the GPS tracking system was working just fine and the weather was perfect. We should be alongside the Coast Guard cutter and the *Bordereau* right on time—before 10 a.m. Fox sat in front of deck-mounted binoculars like a kid squealing with delight as she pointed out the occasional lone whale or pod of dolphins. Ernie had custom-created a swivel mount for the Steiner 20x80 Military Binoculars. They were as good as any I'd seen.

At 9:50 a.m. Fox yelled out, "I see the Coast Guard boat!"

Ernie said, "Let me see," and took the post. Looking through the glasses he said, "About twenty-five miles. Half hour at the most." Looks like she's about eight to ten miles off the coast of Cuba."

Fox sat back down and resumed her position as binocular attendant to the amusement of the others on deck. "So that's Cuba!" she said. "Hmmph; short distance from Florida."

"Really fast boat, Ma'am," Ernie beamed.

Ten minutes later Fox announced, "Another craft is approaching the *Bordereau,* this one coming from shore. Probably the Cuban Coast Guard," she concluded.

"There is no Cuban Coast Guard," laughed Henry. "They have a couple of Russian-built patrol boats and that's it. But this is probably a big enough deal they've sent one out to nose about."

"We may be able to solicit their help," I suggested.

"Just how can they be of any help?" Henry asked.

"Looks to me like the *Bordereau* is well within Cuban territorial waters, which means any infractions of international law may fall under Cuban jurisdiction," I answered. "I suspect we may be able to negotiate with the patrol regarding the crew; remember, only ten were supposedly on board. Where did the other nine come from? We know they boarded in Key West, but Watters and Hendricks ignored every known protocol. You want all the U.S. personnel and any contraband, but Cuba can deal with the boat and all the others . . . right?"

"Interesting thoughts, Garrett. Not sure I agree with your conclusion, but it is plausible. I suppose we'll know in a few minutes."

We kept in direct communication with the U.S. Cutter. They had picked us up just moments before Fox saw them. They had been talking to the Cuban patrol boat for more than ten minutes.

"They want to know why we've stopped the cruise ship in their waters," the captain said.

"You told them, right?" Henry asked.

"Yes, Sir," she said. "By the way, Sir, a few things you should know. We have found no other persons on board, but Sir, we found a space below decks where it seems some people have been held in constraints against their will. We found a cabinet in that room with several sets—probably fifteen—of handcuffs and legcuffs. To be blunt, Sir, the room smells of urine and sweat. I believe they were transporting prisoners or trafficking.

Also, Ranger discovered a sizeable cache of heroin in a hidden compartment under a bunk in the crew quarters.

And last, we searched a room which the five on board without passports are calling a boiler room. They have set it up as a work-space to crack that code for the captain . . . or now, as Mr. Garrett has explained, AFOSI.

We had no reason to correct the Coast Guard captain at this point. Ranger, I learned, was a German Shepard sniffer dog on board the Coast Guard cutter.

"Good for Ranger, Captain," Henry said. "Welcome the Cubans aboard. Explain that under maritime law we had suspicions of contraband as well as Americans on board illegally. We'll be there shortly. In the meantime, invite their officers for coffee."

32

Thursday, October 10
In Cuban Waters

Ernie guided *My Second Choice* alongside the Coast Guard cutter; I grabbed a rope that was cast and tied it off. After I dropped a couple of fenders, I tossed ropes to both stern and bow to a cutter crew member; he secured the boats together.

The Cuban patrol boat was anchored some forty yards from the *Bordereau.* A small contingent from a dingy was already aboard the Coast Guard cutter as we climbed aboard.

"Ahh, Commander Waite, my friend, so good to see you," the Cuban officer stuck his hand out, greeting Henry.

"And you, Commander Romero. I was hoping to see you out here today," Henry smiled.

He turned and explained that he and Capitan de Corbeta (Lieutenant Commander) Romero had a five-plus year history of shared responsibility protecting the water between Cuba and Florida.

"Before we board the yacht, Commander, allow me to give you a personal tour of our cutter. You've not seen this class before have you?"

"No, I have not. I'm looking forward to a tour, my friend."

Almost a half hour later, midst "ooohhs and ahhhs" the two returned to the deck. Commander Romero laughingly lamented that his patrol boat was so ancient it was held together with silicone rubber, paint and duct tape.

The U.S. Commander turned to the captain, "How many do we have on board already, Johns?" he asked.

"We have six crew on the yacht guarding those shackled to the rails, Sir," she answered.

"I think it's time we board the yacht."

He started with the chief Cuban officer. "Commander Romero, Captain Johns, Mr. Garrett, young lady, you and you," he said to two Cuban sailors, "join us please."

As we climbed aboard Captain Bosignion was screaming, "I keep telling you, the heroin is a plant. Your men put it under the bunks before you turned your search dog loose in there."

"The U.S. Coast Guard has no interest in the heroin we found." Henry responded with equal volume. "Neither are we interested in the guns we found on several of your crew members and in your quarters.

We leave that for the Cuban authorities. What we are interested in are the murders committed in Key West, undocumented persons aboard your yacht, and the team working on the coded files. Any one of those three can and will carry capital punishment."

Turning to Romero, Henry asked, "Do you have anything to add, Commander?"

"Yes. Guns carry a minimum of ten years each, and there are how many? Twelve? Yes, twelve. The heroin will put you behind bars for twenty, and the confiscation of your vessel is certain."

"So you see," I said to the yacht captain, "whatever bargaining chip you are going to try will not work out well for you."

"How about if I tell you where the boy is?" Captain Bosignion looked beaten, but hopeful.

I didn't bite. "Fox," I said, trying to ignore Bosignion, "take a good look at everyone chained to the rail. Start with the captain, here. Tell me if you recognize any of them."

"I don't remember her, or him, or him, or her," Liz started down the row, "but this one I remember, and this one. They were with the Captain Bosignion in *the Hungry Pelican*."

"Is the Boss here?"

"No. I only saw him the one time, but I'm sure."

"Hey!" yelled a woman shackled at the far end of the rail. "I need to pee! We've all been standing here for hours. Can we all have a pee break?"

"Just as soon as we finish with some preliminary questions of each of you!" Henry yelled back.

He turned to me, "Garrett, start with her. Ask your questions, then escort her to our cutter so she can have a pee."

"What's your name?" I asked the anxious one.

"Claudia Abrogono."

"Why are you on the yacht?" I continued.

"I work on the yacht," she answered in Spanish.

"What are your duties?"

"Whatever the jefe (boss) needs me to do, I do it."

"Who is the boss, Claudia? What's his name?"

"Jefe is just jefe," she said. "I don't know his name."

"If the boss asked you to shoot someone, would you do it?"

"If I don't, he would shoot me," she said without hesitation.

"Have you shot anyone recently, Claudia?"

This time she hesitated, then said, " I need to pee real bad."

"Just one more question, Claudia. Who else on this boat works for Jefe? Point them out to me."

She pointed at four people, one after another--Antonio, Captain Bosignion, Nicolas and the lady at the other end. "Him, him, him and her," she said. "Now can I go?"

I motioned to the female guardsman holding a weapon on those shackled to remove the cuffs from Claudia and escort her to the cutter. Then I moved on to Nicolas.

No, he hadn't killed anybody either. The boss did most of his own killing, but Nicolas had acted as body guard and threatened or beat people who were non-compliant. He had neither seen the young man nor knew of his whereabouts. I released him to another guardsman for transferring to the cutter. I turned to Antonio.

"I'm a private investigator," Antonio began. "The Boss has been a client off and on for three or four years. Strange, because I've never met him.

Everything we've done is by thumb drives or phone calls. He asked me to find some code breakers for a project he was working on. I brought Joyce, Bette and Gabriel together in Miami and was going to leave and go back to Chicago, but I got a phone call from the Boss asking me to bring them down to a cafe in Key West.

There we would meet Captain Bosignion and I would receive payment. The three with me were to work for the Boss, while I would enjoy a cruise aboard his yacht."

"So you met the Boss?"

"Oh, No! Just instructions and promises."

"Did you get paid?"

"Yes, I received cash."

"What do you know about the young lad that was kidnapped?" I asked him.

"Sorry, I know of no such person."

"And the lady at the far end?"

"I was told she is the procurement person. She buys food and supplies for the yacht."

"Fair enough. We'll talk further unless the FBI takes you off the Coast Guard's hands." I turned my attention to Captain Bosignion.

"So you can tell me about the boy. Where is he?"

"You get nothing from me without some kind of concession!" the captain shouted.

"I see." I said, raising an eyebrow. "Who is the lady chained at the end?" I asked.

" Louisa? I couldn't run the yacht without her," he replied. "She came with the yacht when I took it over. She buys and plans all the meals, buys paper products, liquor, everything really."

I nodded appreciatively. "Curious she has no passport." Then I responded to the Captain's "concession" demand.

"Not for me to discuss any deals. Right now I can guarantee you are under arrest by the Cuban authorities on a number of charges; you will be thrown into a maximum security facility, your yacht now belongs to the Cuban military to be disposed of as Cuba sees fit.

When the Coast Guard cutter returns to port you will be charged with kidnapping in a U.S. court. When the Cubans are finished with you for narcotics charges, you will be extradited to the U.S. for kidnapping."

I turned to Henry. "I'm finished with those we consider culprits, Sir." Then I pivoted to look at the Cuban officer.

"Commander Romero, I'm told the female shackled at the end is the boat's procurement officer. She is European, holds no passport. I suspect she procures more than food and drink. U.S. Guardsmen found a small berth full of shackles. I also suspect the Saudi's are either buyers or sellers of human flesh . . . but that's just a guess. If the Commander has no objection we'll take her on board the U.S. cutter."

"No objection from me," Henry said, nodding. "Interesting request. I'm not sure why, but she looks a bit familiar."

"Just a hunch, Henry. If she's that important to the Boss, she may be instrumental in trafficking or drug procurement."

I went on, "I do wish to speak with two Brazilian crewmen for a moment. I believe them to be simply innocent mariners. I may be wrong. I'd like to question them if I may."

"No problem, Señor Garrett. Only two? Does it matter which two?"

"Yes, Sir. I met them a few days ago."

I walked down the row of those shackled and tapped two men. A guardsman released them to me. I set them at a table and motioned for Romano, Henry and Fox to join us.

"Gentlemen and Fox, this is Juan and his friend, Tomas. I met them as they were boarding the *Bordereau.*"

The two sailors greeted the officers with nervous laughter.

"Nothing to be alarmed about, Tomas, just a few questions, okay?"

"Si."

"Was there a teenage American lad on board the yacht for just a day or so and then taken off?"

"No, Señor, I don't remember any young man," Tomas said, shaking his head.

"Wait!" Fox said. "I have a picture. Here, this is the young man we're worried about." She showed them the photo she had of Paul Maggorie.

"Oh! Si! Si, Señorita!" Tomas suddenly remembered. "This fellow was on a small zodiac. He came on board for one night only."

"Si! Only one," Juan nodded his head in agreement.

"Then what happened?" Commander Romero asked, showing sudden interest.

"The zodiac came and picked him up," Juan said, but was interrupted by Tomas.

"No! It was a dinghy from a fishing boat. And we had instructions to hold our position until the fishing boat returns, perhaps today, perhaps tomorrow. I think, Señor, the boy is fishing."

"Thank you, men," I said. Then turning to the Cuban captain, I intervened on their behalf.

"Commander Romero, I believe these men are innocent of wrongdoing, as are a few more in all probability. I ask for leniency for them."

The commander looked at me and smiled. "Ahh, you are now their attorney? Very well, they are free to go. I am satisfied that they are only sailors who witnessed what they thought was a common activity. Besides, they carry current Brazilian passports.

I have others with whom I am more curious, as you have suggested Señor Garrett--those with passports from Saudi Arabia, the other Austrian gent, and the two from Cuba with supposed travel documents. Believe me, gentlemen, we shall get to the bottom of their several activities."

"Thank you, Sir. Fox, I think it's time to go." I stood to end the conversation.

"Wait a second, Bossman. How can we find Paul if we leave. Shouldn't we stay at these coordinates to wait for the fishing vessel?"

I turned to Ernie. "Ernie! We have AIS, right?"

"Just like that Coast Guard cutter. And radar."

"See, Fox? Everything is under control."

After a short conversation between Henry and Romero, Henry approached me.

"I'm going back with my guardsmen, Garrett. Our objective was successful--going back with us are the three code breakers who are cooperating.

They tell me they have passports, we'll check that out before we release them, then your two Brazilian friends, and finally two male and two females, probably Americans, all undocumented and all considered hostiles.

Your two Brazilian friends can catch a ride with us, or they can ride with you. They can stay in Florida for up to ten days, then a free flight to Brazil. Romero will deal with the yacht and the others."

We shook hands with the Cuban commander. As his patrol boat prepared to leave he had final thoughts to share, "Someday our two nations shall be close allies."

Henry replied with a friendly smile, "Little steps, Commander."

We in *My Second Choice* waved as the two government boats and the yacht powered away in their two separate directions, leaving us alone on the water. Tomas and Juan decided upon the Coast Guard cutter, which suited everyone on board Ernie's boat.

"So, what's our plan, Bossman?" Fox asked.

"Now we move out of Cuban territorial waters, keeping the yacht coordinates in our cross-hairs. And from there we watch the radar screen for fishing vessels approaching our target. By the time they realize the yacht is missing we should be upon them and rescue Paul."

We sat in the afternoon sun, drinking beer and listening to Sam and Ernie tell their war stories. I had told Pop I would call him when I had a moment . . . I had several.

"Hi Pop. I'm sitting on a boat between Key West and Cuba . . . no, still haven't found him, but we're getting closer. He should show up on our radar any minute, now. No, Pop . . . literally. We're hoping to spot a blip on our radar sometime this afternoon--either a dingy, a zodiac or a fishing charter boat.

Paul is being held captive but thinks he's on a fishing charter. Hopefully, he'll appear this afternoon, but, just in case, we have ten days provisions before we starve."

There were no zodiacs, no dinghys and no blips on the radar. We were alone on the water. So, after four days we decided to pull the plug. It came about this way:

Ernie and Sam rigged up fishing gear for themselves and spent the four days fishing. Liz spent most of her time using the Steiner binoculars, pointing out the occasional pod of dolphins . . . until Sam tied into a sixty-five pound Sailfish. Then she abandoned the Steiner for a fishing rod.

I watched as she let her line out slowly and laughed as, at only about forty feet, she screamed, "I got one!" The rod was, indeed, bouncing up and down crazily, line was spooling out of the reel at a blistering pace. Then my brain acknowledged-- she did in truth, have a real, live fish on the line.

Strange how a person can sometimes doubt the truth even though it stares him in the face . . . so, after four days we decided four days was enough to know we weren't going to see the chartered fishing boat.

On day five before the first rays of the sun rose above the horizon the big diesel engines roared to life and we were off. I called Henry as we headed for Key West.

"Hi, Henry . . . no, no sign of Paul. We spent the time fishing. Ha! Yes, Fox did manage to catch a forty-six pound Cubera Snapper . . . took her over an hour to pull it in. Sam and Ernie caught a couple of sailfish north of sixty pounds.

What? . . . No, I didn't fish. I was studying the mystery thumb drive we took from the yacht . . . no, nothing yet, but some of the notes from our so-called 'experts' are interesting. Wait, what? . . .

Are you sure? Did you get the call numbers of the zodiac? Shit! Why not? Okay, okay, sorry. So it's still in pla . . .

What? When? Oh, no! Oh, I'm so sorry, Henry. See you soon."

"What was that all about, Bossman?" Liz asked.

"On the way back the Coast Guard cutter spotted a zodiac approximately twenty-seven miles from the spot where the yacht was located originally. It made a sudden 90° turn toward Hispaniola."

"Why not call us?"

"They thought we saw it on our radar."

"That doesn't make me happy, Gumshoe. He should have given us a 'heads up'. We could have chased it."

"Right . . . but too late now."

"What was the other thing? I heard your outburst to Henry . . . you know, 'Oh, no . . . I'm so sorry, Henry' . . . etc."

"Evidently three guardsmen and two prisoners were killed on the way back."

"Really! Who? How?" Fox asked, surprised.

"Didn't go into detail. I expect we'll find out soon enough."

* * *

Ten minutes later Sam sang out, "Three blips on radar heading this way, comin' fast."

"Lemme see," Ernie said. "Take the wheel, Sam."

"How far out?" I asked.

"Oh, 'bout twenty-five mile, thirty at most . . . three separate boats runnin' abreast. Help me pull the tarps off the guns, Garrett," Henry said calmly. Who knows?" he laughed, "they may be *friendlys.*"

A few minutes later Fox, who was manning the Steiner once again, let out a whoop. "I see them! Wow! Three rooster tails! They're coming in hot!"

"Ten minutes, Garrett!" Ernie yelled! "They'll be on us in ten! How do you wanna play this?"

"Blow them outta the water!" Sam jumped in, excitedly.

"No! We wait! They make the first move. Hell, they may be racing. If they want to talk, we talk. But if they're here on business we take them out."

"I say we blow them outta the water!" Sam repeated. "They could be pirates!"

"You'll be seeing the whites of their eyes in a couple of minutes," Fox called out, her eyes still glued to the Steiner, "then you can decide."

33

Tuesday, Oct 15
Mid-morning

Sam threw the engine into idle as we watched the three jets scream closer. No way we could outrun them if we tried.

Two of them roared in front us in a crisscross pattern, sending sheets of water, the occupants shouting expletives and laughing as they passed. Then they slowed to a stop behind Ernie's boat. I counted five in one boat and four in the other.

The third boat circled *My Second Choice,* then stopped thirty feet from the bow. A passenger seated in the back produced a power megaphone.

"Nice day for a boat ride, yes, my friends?" He spoke slowly and calmly; the accent wasn't quite Mexican but somewhere in the Americas.

"It's lovely!" I shouted. "Where are you folks going in such a hurry?

"Ah, Señor, we came to find you!"

Sam, brandishing a semi-automatic long gun, yelled, "Well, you found us! Now what?"

"Oh, mi amigos," the fellow said, "we are not your enemies. We are only here to ask for our property back."

Turning slightly I asked Fox to join me at the bow. I lowered my voice, "Is that the Boss?"

"Definitely not, Gumshoe. You saw my sketch. The Boss isn't Hispanic. But I think I recognize him . . . it's been a few days, but I think he's one of the boss' men."

I turned back to the megaphone. "I just checked with the boss; we don't have any of your property, so please move on.

Sam, throttle'er up. Let's continue."

"No!" the megaphone blared. "I'm trying to be nice, Señor."

I motioned for Sam to drop the big engine back out of gear.

"Please! We brought cervesa," their leader smiled, "let's sit like gentlemen and enjoy a drink together."

"Sure," Fox shouted, "bring it on board, but just you and one other."

"And no guns!" Ernie yelled, "just to keep it friendly!"

"Bring your boat in close," I shouted. We'll drop the ladder, then the boat goes back out thirty feet. We'll talk."

They complied. Two men stood and showed they had no weapons. Ernie gripped each by the hand and pulled them up as they came on board *My Second Choice.*

We sat so that our visitors sat with their backs to the water, shielding Fox and me from a frontal attack. Fox kept her Beretta in her lap under her sweater, Ernie and Sam kept the big M-240s trained on the two speed boats off the stern. I was content to keep my weapon in my belt.

"Señor y Señorita, let me introduce myself y mi amigo," Mr. Megaphone said, setting four bottles of Bohemia beer on the table, "I am called Ronaldo, and this is Jaime."

"You were aboard *The Blue Moon* the night she was pulled out to sea weren't you, Ronaldo?" Fox opened a beer and took a sip, waiting casually for the answer.

Smooth question, Fox, I thought, but Ronaldo covered without blinking.

"Oh, no, Señorita. I wasn't anywhere near Key West that night. I was tarpon fishing up near Key Largo. I heard about it, though."

By this time we all had beers in hand. I noticed Jaime's hand shake a bit as he took a sip. Fox's question had clearly unsettled him, but he steadied at Ronaldo's smooth response.

"Now, Señor," Ronaldo said, "let's talk about my property. I must insist that you hand it over to me."

"Explain," I laughed. "I'm willing to listen. If you're right, I'll give it to you. If you're wrong, I insist that you return to your boat and return to wherever the hell you came from."

"The documents and flash drive of course, Señor Garrett."

"Sorry, Ronaldo." I raised my voice. "Whatever documents and USB drives I have are, and never have been yours. Where did you get your information?"

"A good source, my friend. A good source," a broad, knowing smile spread across his face.

I smiled back. "Number one, you are not my friend, Ronaldo. And second, my sources tell me you are a hired flunky for some guy named Jefe. You're just a goon, Ronaldo, just a lackey. You see, I also have my sources. Now get off this boat!"

"You are making a grave mistake, Señor." He stood. His smile was quickly replaced by a dark sneer. "We will blow you out of the water!"

"What did you just say?" I stood, leaned down and put my face six inches from Ronaldo's. "Did you just threaten me and my friends?"

Jaime reached into his inside pocket as Ronaldo raised an arm in the air . . . obviously a signal to fire upon us.

I yelled, "Take'em out, Ernie!" as a knife flashed in front of me. I was able to deflect it.

At the same time, Jaime barely unholstered his weapon; it was just peeking out from his jacket when Fox's Beretta put three holes in his midsection. She backed away as Jaime crumpled onto the steel deck

"Take the throttle, Fox!" I shouted as I wrestled Ronaldo for his knife. "Run over that forward boat if they don't move!"

I could hear the bursts from the big deck guns and the smaller chatter of our adversaries' sub-machine guns as Ronaldo and I fought.

Fox pulled the throttle wide open; the boat in front gave way, it's occupants dropped whatever weapons they had and sat petrified, as their pilot tried to escape the big cutter bearing down on them. Behind us only the M-240 deck guns were blasting away. The jet boat crews were silent.

Meanwhile, my hand to hand with Ronaldo continued. He was small, maybe 150 lbs or less, but he was strong and wiry. I knew some martial arts but he seemed to know every move. One move he used repeatedly was a thrust, spin and kick. I remembered being part of Aikido training as a young military Airman confronting sword or knife-wielders . . . the idea being one should counterattack on the thrust. I could have pulled my weapon and shot him, but I rejected that idea in favor of questioning him or at least taking him back to Florida. Bound. The thought of throwing him overboard was my second choice. If it came to that it would be my first choice.

The thrust came. In a single motion I slapped his arm across my body with my left hand and, turning sideways, grabbed his wrist with my right, throwing him off-balance. The knife went clattering off the deck and into the water as I twisted his wrist backwards. Ronaldo went down on his knees, cursing in pain.

Winds were picking up. A storm was indeed brewing here in the South Atlantic. Sheets of rain were coming with the winds, and swells were growing higher by the minute.

"Ernie!" I called out, "you good?"

"We're fine. Two survivors in the water. Shall we pick'em up or leave'em?"

"Toss them a raft. We'll call it in to the Coast Guard. One of you come up front and take over for Liz on the motor. We need to follow that remaining jet boat. They'll outrun us, but stay as close as you can. Keep them on our radar."

Liz searched through Jaime's clothes for any paperwork, found none, and without ceremony, rolled him into the sea. Then she washed the deck down with a few buckets of water.

I called Henry.

"Commander," I began, "we're on our way in. Should be there in about three hours. Looks like we have a hurricane coming in. I want to make sure Ernie's boat is safe."

"Just plain Henry, Garrett, please. Yes, it's not been classed as a hurricane but certainly more than a squall. Did you get your boy?"

"No, but we ran into part of the crew that has him . . . three jet boats. We are at this moment chasing the only surviving boat with about four on board. Pretty windy out here. Not sure we'll keep up the chase.

We have the leader with us, a fellow named Ronaldo. He made a tactical error . . . and we left two of the hostiles in the water clinging to an overturned boat and a lifebuoy. You might consider picking them up." I gave Henry the coordinates of the short sea battle. I heard him yell to someone to gear up a chopper.

"Be prepared when you get back, Garrett; that FBI lady, Teresa Hughes, met us at the docks and has been in town waiting for you to get back. I told her you would be gone for five or six more days."

"Yeah, well don't tell them we're on our way," Fox smiled.

"Did the FBI take your detainees, Henry?" I asked.

"No, I still have them. They seem harmless enough. We have them under house arrest. Ensign Brady is taking good care of them. See you soon."

We kept the fleeing jet boat on Ernie's radar until it veered off toward the Bahamas. Ten minutes later the blips on the screen increased from one to four, then seven; further chase was pointless. We headed for Key West.

* * *

Henry was waiting for us as Ernie guided *My Second Choice* into her slip. It was a few minutes after 4 p.m. Rain was beginning to pelt the deck, spattering up, leaving puddles here and there in the low spots.

"Looks like you brought the storm with you, Garrett."

"Yeah, I don't think so. More like we were chasing it. So, regarding the shooting on your boat, how did that happen, Henry?" I asked, as I tossed him a line. Fox was right behind me. I grabbed her arm and steadied her from slipping on the slick surface.

"He got the jump on one of my guys as soon as they uncuffed him. Before we stopped him he'd shot two more who were guarding the so-called code breakers and shot one of his own before we shot him."

"Who was he?" Fox asked.

"Antonio, the attorney-recruiter who found them and brought them in on the project."

"Sounds like a direct order from the Boss," Fox suggested.

"Likely," Henry said. "He shot Nicolas, who I understand was one of the Boss's lieutenants, and left the code-breakers alive. I don't think Antonio expected to die. In fact, the guardsman that shot

Antonio said the man was surrendering his gun as he was being shot . . . just a fluke . . . couldn't take the bullet back."

"And the three cryptographers?" I asked.

"As I said, safe in our holding cells." Henry smiled and shook his head. "They were dupes in a bad situation. I was going to pick their brains and cut them loose, but the FBI showed up. I told Hector and the Key West coroner. Bodies have been taken away and my higher-ups have been notified.

I'll be leaving tomorrow at 9 a.m. for two funerals, one up in Bushnell and one in Keithville, Louisiana. Our third boy will be attended by another of our staff. Damn shame I can tell you."

Ernie and Sam had been cleaning out *My Second Choice.*

"What do you want done with your fish, little lady?" Sam asked Fox.

We'd cleaned and gutted Fox's fish, cut it into five large chunks, shrink-wrapped it and put it in an oak cask and dropped it over the side on a cable. Then we'd forgotten about it until now.

"Give it to Henry, here," she answered. "He can bar-b-que it. We'll join his staff for a meal when he gets back."

"Oh, right! Thanks for that, Fox." Henry smiled. "I'll see what I can do. But we can put it into the big freezers we have in our kitchen. My crew might smoke part of it for you.

More importantly, Garrett," Henry continued, "where are you going to stay tonight? Hector kicked you out of Key West, remember?"

"Oh! yeah, I'd forgotten about that," I winked at him. "Hey, maybe we can bunk in your holding cells along with those others."

"Not bloody likely!" Henry snapped. "Maybe you can stay on Ernie's boat. We'll be happy to take that prisoner, Ronaldo, off your hands, though. He can keep the remaining hostiles company."

"Just joking, Henry," I laughed. "No, Fox and I will walk Ronaldo into Hector's jailhouse with a complete report of our confrontation on the water and ask him to join in formal questioning of our prisoner . . . and I'd like to do it before that FBI lady and her cohorts even know we're back.

We'll figure out from there where we'll be spending the night. I have a feeling it'll be *The Chelsea House.*"

I called Hector. Five minutes later a squad car came to pick the three of us up. We said our goodbyes to Ernie and Sam.

"Ernie," I called out, "breakfast at *The Hungry Pelican* tomorrow morning at 6:30? Bring your bill—we'll square up."

Ernie nodded as Fox slipped into the front passenger seat next to Norm Gornich, the rookie cop. I held the rear door open for Ronaldo and motioned for him to slide over to give me room beside him.

"We'll talk tomorrow," Hector said, as Norm locked Ronaldo in a cell. "I'm going home to see my family. It's been a few busy days since you came into town, Garrett. Damn! I was just catching my breath, too, when you called and said you were back." He winked at Fox, "I'll get your story tomorrow. Now get out of here before I change my mind and lock you up."

"*Hungry Pelican,* 6:30 a.m.?" I asked.

"I'll think about it. Goodnight. Oh! By the way, Garrett, your Mustang was towed into our impound. It was torched a couple of nights after you left."

Norm Gornich dropped us off at *The Chelsea House.* Unfortunately, no rooms were available. Jennifer's brother, Munch was at the desk. He had a typewritten list of motels in the area he could recommend. We chose one on the water eight blocks away.

"You're looking good, Munch. How's the shoulder?"

"Better every day, Sir."

Fox's car was still parked in *The Chelsea House* lot, but the first storm surge had abated, we saw enough blue sky to think we could risk walking . . . Mistake. Five blocks along the water, walking turned to running. Before the motel entrance we were blown sideways and drenched to the skin. We entered, laughing.

There were two rooms available. We chose the first one offered.

"You'll need more towels," the gent behind the desk observed with a smile. He handed Fox four large bath towels and me a key card. "We have laundry facilities if you need your clothes washed.

Please use the entry mats to wipe your feet before entering the room. My name is John if you need anything else. Enjoy your stay."

"How about a bottle of Martell?" I asked, with a grin.

"Martell. Is that scotch?"

"No. Cognac."

"AB Liquor on Seafaire. They'll deliver."

The room was comfortably and expensively appointed. Huge, with two king beds, a desk with plush captain's chair, a library wall filled with upwards of a hundred books, many of which were hard bound, and a spa for a bathroom. I set my fedora on an end table.

"I'll take this one," I said, tossing my fedora on the side table to the bed closest the door. I pulled off my holster and dropped my .45 next to the hat.

"I am drenched, Gumshoe," Fox said, shedding her outer garments. "I suppose this room will have to work," Fox said batting her eyes and looking around at the upscale furnishings . . . "so long as you don't peek."

"Hey!" I was literally shocked at the amount of skin she revealed. "Throw a towel around yourself. Keep that up and I will peek . . . maybe even make a video."

"Oh! Goodie, a blue movie, Gumshoe! I'm so excited!" There was a twinkle in her eye.

"Fox! Fox! Enough! Sorry I mentioned it. Grab a book, take a sauna, a jacuzzi, whatever; I need to make some phone calls."

"Awww, Gumshoe. You're a real spoilsport! Not a romantic bone in your body!"

"You and I work together, Fox. You're my subordinate." *Was she serious?* I wasn't going to push the charade any further. I turned my back, took my shirt off, draped a dry towel over my shoulders, sat at the desk and dialed a number, thinking all the time, *was she really serious*?

My first call was to AB Liquor . . . then I called the car rental agency. They already knew. I wrote a check for my deductible.

34

Wednesday, Oct 16
Early morning

A crowd met Fox and me as we arrived at *The Hungry Pelican*. There was Ernie and Sam, Hector and another policeman, Mateo, whom we had met the night of the police headquarters explosion. But the surprise of the morning was Jennifer who arrived with Henry and Fernando. The time was 6:25 a.m.

Joe brought coffee.

"Where's Marge?" Sam asked him. "She only gits Saturdays off. She playin' hooky?"

"She'll be in by 8:00. She had an early morning appointment. What can I get for you all?"

We ordered. After a few wise cracks were shared around the table, Henry opened with a resumé of our recent adventures. He stood.

"A yacht entered our harbor the other day as we all know. When it left we discovered it was tied to Garrett's missing teenager and some valuable military documents. We caught up with the yacht in Cuban waters and turned it over to the Cuban Navy along with a couple of prisoners and some contraband. Garrett was with us in Ernie's boat.

Our Coast Guard cutter headed back with some undocumented, but obvious U.S. citizens. Unfortunately, one of our prisoners overpowered a guardsman and shooting erupted, leaving five dead, including the shooter--Antonio: Nicolas, a cohort, and three guardsmen. The two females, Claudia and Louisa, are being sent today to the Monroe Detention Center here in Key West, and from there bused up to ICE in Miramar to be interrogated for complicity in wrongdoing.

Garrett has more to add." Turning to me he invited comment with, "Garrett."

Henry sat. I felt no compunction to stand so remained seated as I narrated our confrontation with the three jet boats, Sam and Ernie's heroics, the capture of Ronaldo, and his jailing in Hector's jail cell.

"I was hoping to question the two females further, myself. Is it too late, Henry?"

"Yes, I'm afraid so."

At that moment Teresa Hughes walked in. She spied our table, pulled up a chair next to me and interrupted our friendly get-together.

"Why did no one call to invite me?" she demanded.

"Simple," Fox answered just as forcefully, "we didn't wish to invite you. But now that you're here, uninvited, the bill is yours!"

"Which reminds me, Ernie," I said, "do you have my final bill for the fishing trip?"

"Shore do, Gumshoe. Right here."

He passed a folded sheet of paper along the table toward me. As it got to Teresa, instead of passing it on she unfolded and read it. I made no move to take it from her. I simply turned and stared at her.

"I determined the other day that I didn't like you much. Today I double down on that feeling. You are a very rude young woman, Miss Hughes." I held my hand out, "I'll have the invoice, please."

"A bill including $400.00 for guns and ammo? I don't think so! What's this all about?" she demanded.

Sam spoke up, "Respectfully, ma'am, that there is none of your concern."

Henry interrupted, "Call the Cuban Navy. They'll fill you in with details, Miss Hughes. This breakfast table is by invitation only. You may call and make an appointment with Hector, Mr. Garrett or me at a later time. Thank you for understanding."

The FBI agent stood, threw the piece of paper at me, and stormed out. The entire cafe was silent for a full minute as other patrons recognized the obvious animosity hanging like a thick cloud over our table.

Then someone at another table yelled, "Hey! Could I get some service over here, Joe?"

As if on cue the place resumed its friendly chatter.

Joe the waiter came around with our orders.

I could feel Hector staring at me during much of my oration and the FBI disruption. He shook his head.

"Garrett, Gumshoe, whatever your name is, you make enemies as fast as anyone I know, but you are direct. I like that. I've changed my mind about booting you out of town. Stick around a few more days. Do all the investigating you want, but keep me in the loop. Understood?"

"Absolutely. Fox, after you eat, run and get your car, please. Shall we grill our prisoner after we eat, Hector?"

"Sure." Then he asked, "Want to join us, Henry?"

"Can't. Plane to catch in an hour or so. Going to a funeral."

"Oh! That's right . . . I forgot. Couple of questions before you go," I said. "One: still have the code breakers?"

"Yeah, they're there. Just ask Ensign Brady. The others are under arrest in chains and will be transferred to Miramar, possibly on their way . . . maybe even there by now."

"Hmmm, why Miramar?" I asked.

"We checked yesterday. We were told to send them up there. Deportation center; interrogators there are tops."

"Okay. Question two: who else knew our coordinates on the water? Those three jet boats came flying directly at us. Our radar picked them up over twenty-five miles away."

"I've been mulling that over as well," the Commander answered, "I shared your situation with only two others: Hector's office and Ensign Brady."

Hector broke in. "First I've heard of it. Who did you speak with?"

"A man–policeman I assume," Henry shrugged.

Hector looked at Mateo who shrugged and shook his head.

"Eat your breakfast, Garrett. We may be questioning more than your prisoner. Damn! I hate the thought of a mole in my ranks. We lost three officers in that explosion the other night, brought in three recruits and a sergeant from Miami. I think we start there."

We walked out. I called Jennifer over.

"You working for the Guard, now?" I asked.

"Four days a week!" she beamed, "started Sunday the twelfth with guardsman, Francisco Bardos. It's only six hours a day--Tuesdays, Thursdays, Fridays and Sundays. I have school Mondays and Wednesdays, with Saturdays free." Then she added, "I understand you're not staying with us anymore?"

"Good for you, Jen!" I exclaimed, ignoring her lodging question. Fox waited at the curb. I joined her. "Go, Hector? We'll follow you."

We were right behind Hector when his speed doubled, along with lights and siren. We kept pace. Another squad car pulled beside us, an angry officer motioned Fox to back off, then pulled in behind the chief's cruiser as we complied.

Fox looked at me. "Now what do you suppose, Bossman?"

"Keep up with them but give them space. That fellow looked serious didn't he?" I grinned.

"Sure did."

It was only a few blocks, but it became suddenly clear . . . the cruisers were headed for police headquarters!

35

Wednesday, Oct 16
Late morning

Hector opened his cruiser door and hit the ground running. The officer who had cut us off (Oscar Boules, one of the recruits from Miami) tried to block our entry through the double glass doors but Hector shouted, "Let them in!" between expletives!

The police headquarters had been completely remodeled since the explosion of October 8[th,] from jail cells to front doors . . . in a sweeping look around the main foyer I counted three bodies . . . the new desk sergeant just brought up from Miami, her body crumpled over the incoming desk, on the floor was one of the new recruits whom I didn't recognize, and near the door into the new cells was our young friend, officer Norm Gornich.

"Garrett, damn you! This stops now!" he bellowed, pointing at the open, empty jail cell that had once housed Ronaldo.

"Why? How? Who?" his fists were doubled. He slumped into the desk sergeant's chair in anger and frustration, hands covering his eyes. Then he took a deep breath, exhaled slowly . . . and stood.

"What do we have so far?" he asked. It was a rhetorical question to no one in particular this early in the morning in Key West.

"Nothing, Sir," replied the cop who had entered just ahead of us.

"Of course not," Hector agreed. "Ain't reality a bitch? Hell, we're the only ones here."

"Maybe not, Hector," I suggested. "Who called you with the bad news?"

"One of our offi. . . . oh! Who *did* call me?"

"Can we hear the call?" Fox asked.

We all walked out to the Chief's car. He punched replay on his radio tape.

"Emergency!" A male voice. "Officer needs assistance! Respond to base! Please, Th . . Aghhhhh."--followed by a single shot from a handgun.

"So we're back to square one," Fox said with certainty. "The caller didn't escape. That's Gornich." We all agreed. Mateo and another officer entered the station.

"Don't touch anything! Call the coroner," Hector yelled to them. "Get him down here. Get forensics in here, too."

"Boss, we don't have a forensics team here in Key West. They're headquartered in Key Largo."

"Bring them down! Call that FBI gal, as well. Bring her in here!"

"Chief Rodriguez! Hector!" Fox almost shouted to get his attention! "I have an up-to-date DNA/

fingerprint database. Most of what we need is on my laptop. Everyone put on some gloves."

I broke in. "No signs of struggle. Almost looks like your boys knew or were comfortable with the shooter. Small bore hand gun, most likely .22, shooter picked up all the shell casings--nothing to help us there, but dust this whole place. Put results on a flash drive. We can identify anyone who's been here recently if they touched anything.

When the FBI arrives they can help with anything we've missed. Ms. Hughes will feel useful, and any samples her team finds--hair, skin, whatever--can go to an FBI lab."

The coroner team walked in and set to work with the dead. We did the same. Twenty minutes later we had a collection of sixteen clear and different prints--all included in the international database. Our findings included thirteen cops: Hector, Mateo, Tim White, Oscar, Rubin Benites, Shirley Rhodes, Axel Lourdes, Monte Moñez, the four new from Miami (two of them dead still on the floor--along with Norm Gornich), and of course, those of Fox, Ronaldo and myself.

"Who's missing?" Hector bellowed. Without waiting for an answer, he said, "I want everyone in here, now! Everyone! You hear me, Mateo? No exceptions!"

"Chief, that's going to be difficult to do. We just can't muster everyone at a moment's notice."

Hector slumped back in the chair. "Oh, I know, Mateo. I'm just so damn frustrated at the way we're being picked apart. I'd like to say it's all this

California fella's fault, but it's much bigger, I'm afraid.

Garrett, Fox! Don't go home yet! I'm going to need all the help I can get. Raise your right hands, I'm going to deputize you both."

"Whoa, Chief! That can't happen!" I protested. "You know Fox and I are on an assignment. We're getting close and I mean to finish the job. We'll help you all we can, Hector, but I cannot have our efforts compromised by cross-purpose orders."

Hector shrugged. "I didn't think so, but I had to ask."

"May we have the list of your officers, Hector?" Fox asked. "The one with addresses, work and home phone numbers. We'll follow up. Least we can do."

"Good samples of boot prints and tire treads out here as well, Hector," I called to him as I pushed the door open. "The ground is really soft."

"You thinking what I'm thinking, Fox?" I asked as we pulled out of the police parking lot.

"Yes, and Hector did as well. Dirty cop. Let's go knock on some doors. There aren't that many, and they should all be awake and up by now."

We scrolled down the list, crossing off those obviously not involved--the three on the floor and Hector, and vacationing Gary Thune--all others, even Oscar and Mateo who followed us into the station were suspect unless we determine they have solid alibis.

We followed the list as written--alphabetically, but as we walked away from Tim White's door an hour later, we were no closer to finding a murderer among the police.

"Let's pop into the *Pelican.* Maybe someone saw or heard something."

"Hey, Gumshoe! Hiya Fox. Good to see ya," the old fellows club shouted almost in unison as we walked in. Marge waved to us. We scooted in next to a few of them at a table near the door.

"We heard 'bout this mornin', Gumshoe. Turrible shame. Jus' turrible."

"How did you hear?" Fox asked.

"One of the cops called," Fox's old pal, Lenny, volunteered. "He was askin' 'bout you. If you was here, where you was stayin' . . . like he wanted to git ahold of you real bad."

Marge came with a full carafe.

"Breakfast?" she asked.

"No, just coffee and a danish for me," I said.

"Same," Fox nodded, flipping a mug over.

I turned to Lenny. "That makes no sense. All the cops at the station know where we are, and we've just been in contact with the others. Why would they be looking for us?"

"He didn't say nothin' 'bout you, Gumshoe. He only asked about Fox, here."

"So, fellas, what did you tell this cop?" I asked, frowning and staring across the table at Fox.

Another old gray hair shrugged, "We couldn't rightly say where you was, cuz we didn't know."

"Yeah, and we don't know where yore stayin'."

Fox sipped her coffee, thinking. "Ronaldo?" she looked at me, holding her mug with both hands, raising an eyebrow.

I nodded. "Ronaldo. We need to be extra careful. He's hunting you, Fox."

We started for the door but turned back as Marge called out, "Garrett! You have a minute?"

We followed her into a supply room away from the restaurant patrons.

"I wanted to talk to you in private," she laughed, "they say loose lips sink ships, and some of the fellas in there say anything to anyone at any time."

I nodded, "We understand completely."

Fox was in agreement. "So what's up?" she asked.

"You know I live next door to Gary Thune, right?"

"Yeah, but he's out of the country until next week."

"This Gary Thune . . . that's the cop, right?

"Yes," Marge continued, "he's supposed to be in Britain until the 22nd. Well, as I backed out of my drive Sunday morning I thought I saw his front door close. I dismissed it after a few seconds, chalking it up to shadows, glare, reflections off my glasses . . . I just figured my imagination was running wild, you know?"

"Go on," I encouraged.

"This morning as I walked across to the hospi . . ."

"Wait!" Fox pushed her palm in front of Marge's face, "what time was this?"

"Around 7:30 a.m. I had a 7:45 appointment at the hospital. Anyway, Gary's house was dark, all was serene. But, when I walked back at about 8:10 there were fresh, muddy tire tracks in his drive. No car, no signs of life, nothing else . . . just the tracks."

"Were there shoe or boot tracks on his front steps?" Fox asked.

"Not to my knowledge, but I didn't walk over there to snoop further. I don't know what it means, but I think someone is going in and out of Gary's house."

"So do I. Thanks, Marge." I dialed Hector's cell phone.

The rain that had pelted us last night and very early this morning had finally subsided. Patches of blue sky were expanding . . . the sun warming. It felt good.

"Hector, Garrett here. Did your team make plaster casts of tire treads or boot prints at your headquarters? . . . No? Are you still there? . . . Okay, take lots of pictures–tires and footprints. Meet me at Gary Thune's home in twenty minutes . . . Yes, his home, across from the hospital. Bring your dusting powder as well . . . I'm not sure, but . . . as I said, not sure . . . something Marge just told me . . . I'll explain when we meet up . . . 11:00? Yeah, 11:00's good . . . see ya."

36

Wednesday, Oct 16
11:00 a.m.

The Thune driveway was indeed covered in recent muddy tire tracks. There were also shoe tracks, two sets--one smaller going up and down the steps, the other, larger, coming down the steps only. Runners.

Fox took picture after picture using her digital camera. I tried the front door. Locked.

We leaned against her rental car in Marge's driveway and waited for Hector. It was still a bit early. We killed the time discussing several topics including the two sets of shoe tracks, the murders in the jail, the jailbreak itself, the whereabouts of young Paul . . . but we avoided the "elephant in the room" . . . Ronaldo seeking to know the whereabouts of Fox.

"So, Marge lives across the street from the hospital and next door to a policeman. Sounds like the perfect situation," Fox smiled.

"Let's hope so," was all I said as I spotted the Chief's cruiser pull around the corner. Fox ran to make sure he didn't pull into the Thune driveway; she motioned for him to park at the curb.

"So what's the problem, Garrett?"

"Take a look at the driveway, Hector."

The Chief walked just far enough to see the fairly large, fairly new tire tracks and the shoe imprints on the thin film of mud on Thune's driveway.

"Oh! I see!"

"And," Fox noted, "whoever pulled in, pulled back out to continue in the same direction. He wasn't turning around."

"Um-huh, got it, young lady. Looks like someone swung by just long enough to pick up something . . . money, passport, person. What else you got?" He was now interested.

We filled in the details of Marge's suspicions, and the window of time the muddy prints were made—coinciding with the deaths at the jail and the Gornich call for help.

"You have powder for fingerprints, Hector?"

"Of course." He produced a ziploc bag of powder. He handed her the bag and a soft brush.

"I've never done this before, Chief," Fox declared, handing it back. "I don't want to screw it up. If there are good prints I can take the pictures and identify whose they are, but please, you do the dusting. I'll watch."

Hector walked to the door, dusted it and the rails for prints. He found several. Fox took pictures and hurriedly loaded them into her computer.

Hector whistled at the results: Ronaldo's prints were everywhere: on the door handle, on the rails, on the window sill. My prints were also clearly visible on the door handle, but that was to be expected.

"Last thing I want to tell you, Hector, is that someone, probably Ronaldo, called *the Hungry Pelican* at about 8:30 this morning asking the whereabouts of Fox, and wanted to know where she's staying while she's in town."

"Because I can identify someone from that night I was tied up on *The Blue Moon*," Fox interjected, "someone who's in hiding, and can't show his or her face because it's so familiar."

"You're saying someone perhaps like Thune." Hector nodded . . . pretty damn sad, if true.

"Look at the facts, Chief. Why did Ronaldo stop here? Fox has never seen Thune. Her life was threatened several times while she was hospitalized."

"Do you have a picture of Thune at your Command Post?" Fox asked.

"Command Post? I like that," Hector smiled. "Yes, we have several photos of personnel at our command post, including an 8 x 10 of each staff member. Let's go take a look."

37

Wednesday, Oct 16
12:00 noon

We were met by Tim White and the three Feds when we walked through the doors. No other cops were in the office.

"Are you the only one here, Tim? Damn! When I left a while ago there were three officers here. From now on, I want no fewer than two in the Command Post at all times. You hear?"

"Chief," Tim protested, "we were three until this crowd walked in," nodding to the FBI crew, "then Oscar and Miguel felt it was okay to go back out in the field."

"Whatever!" Hector continued. "Tim, bring me that personnel binder under the Duty Desk. It's the red one with glossy pictures."

Hector handed the red binder to Fox. "Take your time. Have a good look at my officers. If you see anyone who was involved in your kidnapping the night *The Blue Moon* was pulled out of the harbor let me know."

Fox sat at a desk, carefully turning pages. She suddenly sat bolt upright.

"It's him, Gumshoe! It's him! . . . the one they call *The Boss*."

She slammed her fist on the 8 x 10 glossy of Gary Thune that stared at her from a page in the binder. "This is the monster that tried to kill me!"

"That son-of-a-bitch! Sitting here right under my nose! Murdering his co-workers with disdain. White! Put out a BOLO for him. If he offers resistance, pump him full of lead!"

"I wouldn't put it out over the wire, Hector," I cautioned. "He has a scanner for sure. He'll go undercover or disappear for good."

"I don't give a shi . . ."

"Chief Rodriguez!" exclaimed Teresa Hughes, "Mr. Garrett is correct, much as I hate to say it. Better if you place individual phone calls. No sense in arousing suspicion."

"Thank you, Ms. Hughes . . . Chief, Fox and I can call your whole crew. We have names and numbers."

"Do it then, but make sure you tell them what I said; take no prisoners! Kill the son-of-a-bitch...he doesn't deserve a trial."

"That will cost you your job, Hector, if it plays out that way," Teresa cautioned.

"Why? He's not worth one friggin' meal at taxpayers' expense!? I say waste him!"

Fox and I made quick work of making cautionary BOLO calls to the police personnel. Our calls were terse and to the point, asking for no radio contact between units--cell phone only, the capture of Thune and Ronaldo if possible, deadly force if necessary.

"Gumshoe," Fox asked, "do you think we should call the Coast Guard with a BOLO as well?"

"Good thought, Fox. Definitely! Call Henry. They're on a different frequency, too, so they can use their radios to communicate."

Henry wasn't in. Fox's call was transferred to Lieutenant Commander Martaise. Fox had her cell on speaker so all in the room could hear.

"Oh! Hello, Miss McConnell. Henry, as you know, is attending funerals today. How can I help you?"

"I'm sending you some pictures in a few minutes, Helen. They are of two men who have plagued the Key West area of Florida all month. We need you to be on the lookout for police officer Gary Thune and his henchman on all the Florida waterways. Arrest them on sight; if they resist, you are authorized to use whatever force necessary."

Two minutes later, Miss Martaise called back.

"I received your pictures. I'll send BOLOs out to our fleet all throughout Florida and Georgia.

By the way, Warrant Officer Fernando overheard our conversation. He has a listing of Medline Zodiacs he keeps forgetting to give you and Garrett. He says to send it to you, but I can't make out his hen scratching; if you have a minute come pick it up. He's here right now. Want to speak with him?"

"I do," I said, and took over the conversation. When Fernando took the phone, I said, "Thanks for remembering. Fox and I will swing by and pick the list up. Are the three code experts still there?"

"Yeah, Henry was hoping you could interview them before we spring them. Will you have time?"

"Yes. Thank you. We'll be there soon. Give us a few minutes." I ended the call.

"Let's go," I said to Liz. "We'll pick up that list of zodiacs and see if the three can give us any useful information before they return to wherever they came from."

"What are you two planning?" FBI agent Hughes asked, sounding more interested than hostile. I was impressed. But I was more impressed by Fox.

"Wait a minute, Gumshoe," Fox said. Turning to the chiefcxx she continued, "Hector, did you make casts of the tire tracks from early this morning?"

"Sure did, pictures, too."

"Here are the photos I shot from Thune's driveway. Let's compare."

We laid the photos out on a table against the cast.

"Miss Hughes, I'm sure you have the equipment to identify tire tracks, am I right?"

"Absolutely."

"What vehicle does this tire come from?" Fox asked.

A few minutes later Teresa read an FBI report:

"That's a Pirelli Scorpion. It comes standard on a 2019 Mercedes SUV, the AMG-G-63."

"Well, well, guess what?" Hector said. "Gary just happens to have a 2019 Mercedes SUV in metallic red."

Hector turned to Tim. "Get hold of someone out of the Key Largo precinct. Send them a copy of those pictures and have them set up a road block south of town. Take pictures of all passing through and stop any Red Mercedes. Same message: no radio contact with our boys . . . phone only."

Teresa smiled, and seemed pleased with her contribution, "I have teams throughout the Southeastern quadrant. We have our own frequency. I'll send out a BOLO to all FBI agents."

"That will be helpful, thanks," Hector said. "We need all hands on deck to catch that bastard."

"Okay, now can we go see the Coast Guard, Fox?" I laughed.

"Yes, I'm finished, Gumshoe. We can go now."

Hector walked us to the door. *"If you get the chance, Gummshoo,"* he whispered, exaggerating my pseudonym, *"shoot that son of a bitch!"*

38

Wednesday, Oct 16
2:40 p.m.

Lieutenant Commander Helen Martaise was chatting with Ensign Brady at the front desk as we entered the Coast Guard facility.

"Ah, here you are, Mr. Garrett, Fox," she said, holding out her hand. I expected you earlier, but I think the coffee is still hot. She pointed to a carafe and two mugs on the adjacent counter. Fox filled them and handed one to me. There were several comfortable chairs . . . we chose two.

"I'm assuming you heard what happened at the police station this morning about the time some of us were enjoying breakfast at *The Hungry Pelican*," I began, placing my fedora on my knee, while taking a sip of coffee.

"No. Only that you sent over those pictures and told us to watch all the waterways. Tell us," she smiled.

Fox filled her in with the details.

"Three more policemen killed?" Ensign Brady gasped. "That's awful! And you think Gary Thune is involved?"

"Oh! We know he's involved," Fox assured her. "Make sure you wear your sidearms while this man is on the loose. He's vicious; pure evil." She finished her coffee and set the mug on the floor beside her.

"Brady," Lieutenant Commander Martaise pointed to the microphone in front of the junior officer, "make the announcement: everyone strap on their sidearms. I have a feeling these two are serious.

Now, here's the list of Medline Zodiacs, but after you sent those pictures I don't think you need to look too far." Martaise had circled the fifth one on the list—it was registered to Beverley (Bunny) Thune.

I studied the list. Martaise was certainly right about Fernando's writing. It was a good thing the Lieutenant Commander circled number five.

"Nails that down. One more thing. We'd like to spend a few minutes with the three you have in lock-up."

"The code breakers? They're around here somewhere," Ensign Brady laughed, "but they're not in lock-up. We only put prisoners in lock-up.

You'll probably find them in the garden. Go straight down the corridor; hang a left at the second hallway. The door at the end opens to the gardens."

As we walked down the corridor, Fox clutched my arm. "Gumshoe! Thune's wife is mixed up in this! The tug captain, that Turner fellow . . . he said the guy in the zodiac yelling that night could have been a woman."

"Thinking the same thing, Fox. We're on the same wavelength." I squeezed her hand as we hurried on.

There were several benches in the garden facing each other. The three code-breakers were sitting together, chatting, as we had been told. Fox and I joined them.

"I understand you will be leaving us very soon," I said. "I'm sorry I've forgotten your names." We re-introduced ourselves to Joyce, Bette and Gabriel.

"Quite an adventure, right?" Fox asked them.

"We were just discussing that," Bette said, "almost a full month wasted, and now we're going home without jobs."

"That's what greed does to a person," added Gabriel. "We were promised the moon at the end of the project, and now look at us--the best part has been the food the last three or four days."

"I need to pick your brains . . . just a couple of questions if you don't mind," I said.

"Anything in it for us . . . like a reward?" Bette asked, hopefully.

"Ha! More like getting off easy for your part in a kidnapping scheme that has cost the lives of more than twenty people--mostly innocents."

"Are you serious, Sir?" Bette asked.

"As serious as a gunshot wound," Fox answered for me.

"What can we tell you?" Joyce asked.

"The fellow that hired you, remember his name?"

"Antonio," Gabriel answered, "but he's dead now."

"No, I know that. But tell me the story of how he found you and where he took you. Like, how did you get on the yacht?"

Joyce responded, "I answered an ad for a cryptanalyst. I was impressed at the proper request, so answered his ad." The others nodded in agreement.

"Then what happened?"

"We all joined up in Miami with Antonio, a guy named Dario, that woman, Claudia and a couple of others," Gabriel began. "They laid out the job: working on a yacht to decipher a code for their boss. The pay was to be $100,000, split three ways. We were put up in a four-star hotel and the next morning were driven to a remote area on the water not far from here."

Joyce chimed in, "We sat at a table for about a half hour, then along came one of those zodiac boats with the big boss and his henchman named Roberto or something like that."

"Ronaldo," Gabriel corrected. "It was Ronaldo not Roberto . . . and we were sitting on a barge. One of them asked a question of one of the guys in our party . . . his answer didn't satisfy the newcomers, so one of them shot him."

Liz produced the two pictures she had tucked in her purse. "Are these two the two you're speaking about?" she asked, unfolding the pictures.

All three nodded.

"That's Ronaldo!" Joyce blurted out. "He's the one that shot the other fellow."

"The other one is the Boss," Bette agreed. "He ordered it."

"We've met both of these men. Both are very dangerous," Fox verified.

"Then," Bette continued, "we were driven to the dock at 2:15 p.m. the same day and walked aboard the yacht."

"Wait, wait." I said. "Go back to the remote area with the zodiac. Can you describe it more?"

Gabriel spoke, "Give me a pencil and paper. We can probably draw a map if we put our heads together."

"I have a better idea," Bette piped up. "Let's jump in your car and go there together."

"Good idea. But there's room for only two in my car. One of you will have to stay here," Fox said.

"I'm happy to stay," Joyce spoke up. "You two go."

We headed off the main road onto a gravel road about six miles north of Key West. Both Gabriel and Bette thought it about right. But a minute later, they agreed it was wrong, and there must be another road.

Another mile, another gravel road to the left. The only signage was on the main road--Highway 1--and we were skirting a marshy, swampy piece of water called Old Finds Bight. We took the road.

"This looks right," Bette said after a few moments.

Fox drove another half mile or so; another dirt road veered off to the left; we took that one. Soon a maze of dirt roads met us going in various directions.

"I think this is right, but I'm a bit confused," Gabriel admitted, "too many dirt roads."

"That's alright," I assured him. "If you're sure we're on the right road we'll pursue it further tomorrow. Looks like fairly fresh tire tracks, but looking at the sky, it will be dark soon. Anyway, if there's gunfire I don't want civilians involved. Anything else you can tell us before we let you go?"

Gabriel thought for a moment, "No, except there was a big tarp on that barge that provided shade for us."

"What color was it?" I asked.

"Multicolored, like army camouflage."

"Oh!" Bette piped up, "there was a *No Trespass* sign that said the land was privately owned."

"That could be really helpful, thanks," Fox said.

We dropped them off at the Guard compound.

I turned to Fox, "Now, how might that information be really helpful?"

"I don't know, Bossman, but it might . . . right?"

I laughed, "I don't know about you, but I'm not really hungry."

"I'm not either," she agreed. "Maybe some junk food and something to drink."

We drove to a nearby liquor store. Fox walked along the small confectionery aisle and seemed to agonize over her choice . . . chips or donuts, finally ending up with both. I bought the only two bottles of Martell on the shelf. It was 5:15 p. m. We drove back to our new luxury motel.

"Long day, Gumshoe," Fox said, sinking into a comfortable chair. "We're getting close, though, I can feel it. What do you think? Tomorrow?"

"If we're blessed with a miracle, yes," I smiled, pouring two ounces into her upraised glass. "But remember, Fox, our goal is Paul." I brushed the hair away from her eyes.

"Ronaldo and Gary Thune are police business. If they get in our way, they become our temporary objectives only."

"That's why I love you, Gumshoe. You're so logical, practical and brilliant."

"I think what you mean is that I'm just plain bullheaded and determined to do things my way."

Fox continued, "I'd make a good partner for you, you know. I can tell you appreciate my quick thinking, I'm resourceful, resilient and tough, Alan. Maybe not as tough as you, but I'm a tough cookie."

I poured myself a like amount of Martell and sat in the swivel chair I had claimed the night before.

I winked, "It's nice to know I'm loved, Fox."

There was nothing about her statement that was amusing, but rather, a passionate, sober appeal for consideration.

"And," Fox went on, "to balance the scales, Gumshoe, I would and will be a perfect choice for you in the area of affection and passion."

I sat trying to determine how to answer or enjoin her in conversation, but she precluded any of my thoughts with the following:

"I'm finished, Bossman. I said my piece. I'll have more Martell later, so I may have more to say, but for now, I'm proud to be working by your side."

She disappeared to prepare for bed. When she returned she was wearing a motel-supplied robe in light blue. She looked lovely.

I made a few phone calls, first to the General, then to Pop, but I couldn't dismiss the thoughts Fox had crammed in my head. How could I?

"Come and keep me company, Gumshoe," she said, sitting on her bed, patting it. "I have Cheetos."

I laughed and joined her. We watched the trilogy of Chicago Med, Fire, and PD. sharing donuts, Martell and Cheetos.

"Gumshoe, I've been thinking about that call from Ronaldo to the restaurant this morning. Do you think we should be overly concerned or do you think they're on the run, and we have nothing to worry about?"

"There's always a concern, but so long as we're prepared, we'll be fine."

At eleven I showered, brushed my teeth, and returned to my own king-size bed, dressed only in my blue, long-legged boxers. Fox simply smiled at me as I tucked myself in.

"Goodnight, Fox. Try to keep the noise down."

I turned toward the wall. Fox turned the volume down slightly and continued to watch the news, after which she walked into the bathroom to make her final preparations for the evening.

While she was occupied I shed the boxers, putting them on the night stand under my .45--just as I had done the previous night. I haven't worn pajamas since a youngster, and I wouldn't begin any time soon.

As I listened to the last of the local Miami news, Fox opened the door and turned off the bathroom light. The weather girl announced light to moderate rain for the morning hours.

Fox whispered, "Rain tomorrow, Gumshoe. You'll have to wear something more than your blue boxers."

"Right," I agreed, "I'll strap my gun on." Then in a reflex action, I raised my head slightly, opened one eye and glanced at the side table where my .45 lay within easy reach.

"And, Sweetie, make sure you wear your hat."

"Nite, Dear," I said. "By the way, they're Hanes."

She turned off the TV in the middle of the sports report--a bit upsetting to me; the Dodgers were in the National League playoffs. It would have been nice to have heard how they were doing, but I voiced no complaint.

As she slid between her sheets, Fox said quietly, "G'night, Alan."

I was awakened just after midnight; Fox had slipped in beside me and curled her body around mine. She mumbled something about being frightened. I reached around, took her hand, drew her closer; I didn't feel any fabric against my backside . . . she felt good. We slept soundly.

* * *

I woke to Fox's soft rhythmic breathing. She still had an arm draped over my left side. But something else had awakened me--another sound--this one coming from outside . . . the sound of tires on gravel.

I slipped out of bed, trying not to disturb Fox; she stirred only slightly as I pulled my boxers on. An electric clock on the dresser with big, red block numbers told me it was 3:17 a.m. No one should be up and around so early . . . except a baker, and I felt sure whoever was outside was no baker.

I walked to the front of the room and put my ear against the door. The noise of tires against gravel stopped; the faint sound of doors opening and closing followed. *More than one door, Gumshoe. That's not good.*

On either side of the front door, blackout curtains provided total darkness and privacy. *That's good, Gumshoe . . . for now.*

I called the Police headquarters--whispered our location to the officer on the desk--asked for immediate assistance. I was a little too loud. Fox sat up.

"What's going on, Gumshoe? Who were you talking to?"

"*Shhhhhh!*" I whispered and ran back and put my hand over her mouth. "Someone's outside." I continued to whisper. "Go get dressed. Take your Beretta with you. Don't come out until I give you the all clear."

Dutifully, Liz sprang from the bed for the bathroom. I crouched down behind the swivel chair and waited for the police. A couple of minutes passed. *Where are they?*

I went back and again put my ear to the front door. I heard a whispered, "estas listo?" from just outside the door. What did they mean, *Are you ready?* I backed up, just in time to avoid a door slam into my ear.

All hell broke loose. Ronaldo was the first through the door, followed by two other thugs. He carried a 12 gauge. Three blasts from his shotgun destroyed Fox's king size bed before I put two .45 slugs in his head and two more in his body as he went down. The shotgun came flying my way.

The other two were peering desperately into the darkened room for me. I heard a siren, but I could only think of the danger in front of me. I emptied my revolver, dropped one of them, and I think I nicked the other. I grabbed the shotgun, but the fellow ran, leaving the car in front of the unit in the parking lot next to Fox's rental. It was not a red Mercedes SUV.

I tapped on the bathroom door. "All clear."

"Isn't that . . .?"

"Yes, my dear, that is . . . or was, Ronaldo. We're getting closer to finding the Boss."

"Gumshoe! Look at my bed! I could have been lying there in that bed!"

Oscar Boules came through the door. "What the hell happened in here?" he asked, looking around at the chaotic destruction, two bodies and door splintered in pieces by the battering ram.

"Never mind. You're the California private eye aren't you?" Without waiting for an answer he bent over the two bodies. He pointed at Ronaldo.

"That's the prisoner we were holding, isn't it?"

"Yes, and one of his henchmen. There was a third as well. You must have seen him. He raced out of here as you were driving up. I think he's wounded."

"Sure he was on foot, Garrett? I saw no one."

"Yes. Their car is out in front. I don't know which one, but the hood will be warm."

"I did spot a couple of drops of blood on the walkway. I'll check it out. Don't leave just yet."

"I'm only going to disappear to the bathroom to put on some clothes," I laughed.

By the time I reappeared a small crowd had gathered around, including the night clerk, John, who had called the owner.

"Now, Mr. Garrett, the owner will be here soon. I can put you into another similar room, but he may ask you to leave our motel altogether when he sees what you did to this one," John said, shaking his head and smiling.

"Me? I don't mean to bad-mouth the dead, John," I winked, "but you should be directing that accusation to the two fellows over in the corner."

"You'll have to convince my boss. Now let's get you into another room."

We followed John just four units down from our demolished room, set our suitcases down and considered our new room. Other than the 4' x 4' "Jackson Pollack style" abstract between the beds, it's furnishings and appointments were identical.

"You go on back, Gumshoe, you'll need to give them an accounting. I'll put our things away, then I'm going to try to sleep. I'll probably cozy up with my Beretta."

The coroner and another cop, Rubin Benites, were on scene–evidently before chasing after the third culprit, Officer Oscar Boules had called the coroner and Rubin. The shotgun and revolver the two intruders had carried had been put safely in a police cruiser trunk, and I was just giving a deposition to Rubin when Boules returned.

"I followed a blood trail for two blocks before it disappeared on the beach," he said. "So it looks like you winged him, alright."

39

Thursday, Oct 17
6:10 a.m.

Breakfast at *The Hungry Pelican*. Smiling up at us were three officers: Chief Hector Rodriguez, FBI Agent Teresa Hughes and Officer Oscar Boules. Fox scooted in beside Boules on one side, I sat on the end, across from the FBI team leader.

"Little excitement this morning, Garrett?" Hector asked.

"You might say that. Wasn't much fun," I replied.

"The room was pretty shot up by that scatter gun," the Chief continued, "especially the bed. Good thing you got the jump on them."

"Yes, you have my report; it's all there."

"Tell us again, anyway," Ms. Hughes was quick to respond, "you shot and killed three men. Which one of them shot up the bed?"

"I beg your pardon!" Fox became suddenly livid with the tenor of Teresa's question. The innuendo was startling.

I gave Fox's arm a light squeeze, and smiled at her. She was claws out . . . then I focused on Teresa Hughes. Our eyes met. Hers weren't warm and toasty.

"You're not accusing me of setting a trap and wiping out Ronaldo and his buddies are you? And by the way," I said, "two, not three. I only winged the third one. Oscar, here, tracked him to the beach and lost the blood trail in the sand."

Oscar corrected me. "He was found an hour later, Garrett. Early morning surfers called it in. I went out with the coroner team and picked him up."

"Your prints are all over the shotgun, Mr. Garrett," Ms. Hughes complained.

"All in my report!" I was now a bit perturbed. "How long have you been a field operative, Miss? Let me buy your breakfast for outstanding police work.

Marge," I called out, "coffee please. Breakfast is on me this morning.

So," I turned to Hector, "all three . . . I had no idea the third one was wounded so badly. I thought I'd only nicked his leg. Sorry a group of surfers were the ones to find him."

The FBI "expert" wouldn't let go, but kept coming back at me from different directions.

"You have been involved in more than twenty murders involving shootings since being in Key West, Mr. Garrett. How do you explain that?"

Marge interrupted us with coffee and took our orders. I handed her my credit card as she walked by.

Back to the FBI agent. "You're wrong on so many levels, Miss, and should stop talking now before you become a bigger embarrassment to the institution. But let me explain the difference between a justifiable homicide and murder. Now, murder is when" . . .

"Enough!" barked the FBI agent, drawing attention to everyone in the dining room.

"As of this morning I'm taking over the search and capture of this rogue police officer, Gary Thune. You will all report to me, Chief Rodriguez.

Mr. Garrett, you will bring me up to date on whatever information you have, and then butt out. You will not pursue Mr. Thune under any circumstances. Is that understood?"

"I will pursue my goal wherever there are bread crumbs, Miss. Should you insist on continuing down your pompous road, I may respond in kind. A few phone calls and you could be sitting behind a desk typing dictated reports of field agents."

"You're so full of shit!" Teresa snarled.

"Try me."

"Interfere, and I will have you arrested for obstruction of justice!" she threatened with a skinny finger pointed at me. She put it away when Marge showed up with the food.

"Do we have to sit and listen to this garbage, Bossman?" Fox asked. "Let's finish up and get out of here. We have a long day ahead."

I wished immediately that she hadn't said that. Teresa picked up on it.

"Where are you two going in such a hurry?" she asked.

"That's none of yo . . ."

I cut Fox off again. "We're following up on a lead. Going out to Old Finds Bight."

"What do you know about Old Finds Bight?" Hector asked. He'd been silent up to this point. "There's nothing out there but alligators."

"I don't know anything about it, but we got a tip, so we're on our way out there."

"Not right away, Bossman. We have a few people to visit and some calls to make before we head out. Let's hurry up with breakfast and blow this place."

"You're right." I stood, motioned to Marge. She came with the Visa bill. After I signed it, I put a $20.00 bill in her hand. Fox and I departed.

* * *

"Where to, Gumshoe?" Fox asked with a smile. as we stepped out into the early morning. "I figure you threw that *Old Finds Bight* information out there for a reason."

With no explanation I said, "Yes, I did. Let's go see Henry for a few minutes. He should be back."

Ensign Brady waved and picked up the phone when we walked in.

"The Commander is in his office," she beamed, "go ahead."

"Good morning to you, too," Fox laughed. We continued down the corridor to Henry's office. He was expecting us.

"Two things, Garrett. One--you took my prisoners for a joyride yesterday . . . not nice; two--you brought them back. Can you imagine the paperwork involved?"

"My advice? Get it done before the FBI comes around," I said.

"What can I do for the two of you?" Henry asked, laughing.

"Out on Old Fines Bight . . . are you familiar with it?"

"Just one of many swamp lands down here on the water. A guy could get lost back in there. Roads criss-cross throughout. Why?"

"Second question: Are you familiar with an old barge with a camouflaged covering sitting on the water in that area?"

"Are you talking about *Oyster Alley*? Huh! I haven't thought about that place in twenty years. The old timers, like Ernie and Sam can tell you stories."

"Can you take us there by boat . . . right now?" I asked.

"Hmmm, unorthodox request, Garrett. What's the hurry?"

Fox broke in, "The FBI team is driving there to check it out . . . they may destroy any clues we might find. They have a different set of priorities."

Henry shifted his gaze to Fox, "And what are their priorities, Miss?"

"Linking Gumshoe and me to all the murders in South Florida."

"Now it's much more interesting. Let's go. We just happen to have a Zodiac."

40

Thursday, Oct 17
9 a.m.
Oyster Alley

The zodiac was fast. We zipped in and out of little inlets as Henry tried to recall the location of Oyster Alley with its old barge.

"So much changes in twenty years, you know, but we're getting close. We've had some rescues in this area, mostly kids in their parent's expensive speed boats flipping over and ending up in the alligator-infested water. We even have a few crocodiles in these waters, more every year."

"I don't want to hear any more, Henry!" Fox shouted over the noise of the powerful motor, "the zodiac can't flip, can it?"

"In a hurricane or forty-plus foot waves in mid-ocean, possibly; otherwise, never . . . unless you lean over the side looking for 'gators, Miss." Henry let out a guffaw at his own comedy.

Fox's mouth dropped. "Oh! that was nasty,

Henry!" she scolded, scooting more to the center of her seat. "Shoot him, Gumshoe!" We were all laughing. Suddenly Henry cut the engine and pointed toward the shoreline.

"Whoa!" he announced. "I think we just passed the entrance into Oyster Alley."

We wheeled the zodiac around, and at a slow speed, entered through an outgrowth of Swamp Cypress trees that provided a half-hidden entry into a cove . . . hence, appropriately, an "alley".

The area was uninhabited. We explored the barge. It was as described, complete with the camouflaged overhead netting, the twin motors--each with heavy tarp covering--but no bodies, alive or dead. It was an unproductive exercise.

"Satisfied?" Henry asked.

"Yes, I suppose so," I said. My shoulders slumped visibly. "I guess I was hoping to find a cubby on the barge where Paul would be tied and held hostage, but it was not to be. I'm almost out of ideas."

"It was too good to be true, Bossman," Fox shook her head, "I was hoping we'd find Gary Thune, tie him up against a tree, light him on fire, and demand he reveal Paul's whereabouts."

"A couple of romantics," Henry snorted. "Let's get out of here."

As we started out of the cove Henry spotted something white snagged on a low tree branch and steered the zodiac toward it. It was the remnants of a shirt.

"Matches what Gabriel told us about a man's nude body tossed in the water around here," I said, "but we'll leave his body for the FBI to discover."

We made a last, dead slow pass about fifteen feet out along the shoreline. Henry frowned and cut the engine.

"See something?" I asked.

"Maybe," he replied. "Do you see that path there at the waterline? It's sort of a drag or swale, whatever you want to call it." We acknowledged.

"A croc made that on his way to the water," he said. "Now, see this other one," he said, pointing at a similar path in the muddy shore. "I thought that was another one, but it is definitely not the same. Let's pull in once again."

For a second time we tied up using a rope attached to the barge, and scoured the area that concerned Henry.

"You're right, Henry! Recent tracks," Fox exclaimed. "Barely visible but definite."

"Good eye, Henry," I added. "Tracks at the waterline means one thing: people coming in or going out."

"Brilliant deduction, Gumshoe, and, by the way, it's actually one of two things."

"Huh? Oh yeah, right."

Henry headed the zodiac back out of the "*alley*", leaving us with more questions.

41

Thursday, Oct 17
11:15 a.m.
Thune's House

"That's your idea, Gumshoe?" Fox asked, "go search Thune's house? Really?"

"You have a better one?" I asked. "We just need a warrant."

We were sitting in *The Hungry Pelican* with Henry and Hector, enjoying pie and coffee. The other two were amused by the friendly banter between Fox and me.

Henry raised an eyebrow. "If you search that house you'd better do it before Hector, here, finds out you broke in."

Hector, thumping his fingers on the table, nodded and said, "Damn right." Then he added, "Make sure you drag him outside before you shoot him. I can't get a warrant for twenty-four hours."

Marge came by with the coffee. She had kept an ear on our table. As she poured a refill, she leaned into whisper, "make sure you take care of business before Miss Hitler comes back from that wild goose chase."

"It wouldn't have been a wild goose chase if we had only found Paul or a clue or something," Fox made a disappointed face, "but we didn't."

"Hey fellas, let's get serious for a minute. I need to find Paul," I declared. "And I'm afraid time and opportunity are fading fast."

"We'll find him, Gumshoe." Fox wasn't entirely convincing, but I appreciated the attitude.

"We're no closer to tracking Thune down, and he was here! He was local just yesterday! Your BOLOs turned up nothing, right?"

"Nope, nothing," Hector grew serious, "and his car is nowhere to be found."

"And I know his boat is still in its slip," Henry volunteered, "because I put a tracker on it."

"And a tracker on his wife's zodiac?"

"No. Sorry," Fox exploded. "Okay, Gumshoe, I'm convinced. Let's go break his door down."

"Okay, you've persuaded me, Fox.

Fellas, we're heading over there." I grabbed my fedora, and we walked out. Behind us, we heard Hector say, "Where are they going?" Henry answered, "Beats the hell out of me."

* * *

Marge had said there was no movement since Wednesday morning at the Thune house, not a rattle of curtains or flicker of a candle.

We walked around the house. Noted double car garage, solid wood front entrance, around back a huge patio door—opening onto a large deck.

"Best way in is the patio door," I suggested. Fox agreed. I continued, "We'll just tap it with a screw driver or whatever you have in the glove box."

"I have just the thing, Gumshoe."

She walked to a flower bed, grabbed a large rock and threw it against the glass.

"Okay?"

"Sure. Worked fine. Wipe the screwdriver off before you put it back in the garden."

While Fox replaced the rock I stepped through the open door. I almost gagged on the tell-tale stench of decayed flesh. I walked out on the deck and immediately called Rodriguez.

"Hector, get yourself and the coroner crew and whomever you have in forensics over at the Thune home. We happened upon an open door and went in to see if there was anyone in need. The smell of death is strong in here. We'll wait."

"No. Get out of there now! If we come there and find you, we'll have some explaining to do to that FBI team. And, don't touch anything, Garrett."

"Sorry, Chief! I need five minutes. That's all I can take anyway, the smell is so bad. I just want a quick look around. If Paul is dead in there I can identify him, and we can leave your fair city . . . just five before you call your guys in, please."

"Five minutes, Garrett, it's 11:57 . . . well, let's say noon, now. You have until 12:05 p.m. then I'm on my way. I'll have Marge say she saw a broken patio door this morning while she was outside watering or some damn thing. That'll keep your snooping ass out of the fire. Now get to it, Garrett."

42

Thursday, Oct 17
Noon
5 minute Raid Ledgers & a cognac

"Don't touch anything, Fox! Take pictures only. We have five minutes, then we'll head back to the motel before Hector shows up."

"That's all I can handle anyway, Gumshoe ... if that."

Gloves on, we entered. Just inside the odor had dissipated with the outside air. The room was tidy, a den or family room of sorts with TV, lounge chairs, the usual. Nothing jumped out at us.

Through a short hallway the kitchen was to the left, and I assumed, the bath and bedrooms off to the right ... we headed right. I poked my head in the bath; satisfied, we opened a bedroom door. The stench was almost overwhelming; Fox walked outside for a breath of fresh air.

There were two twin beds, a young dead woman in each, with bullet holes in their heads. One four-drawer dresser, empty. Nothing else in the room. I took pictures and moved on.

Second bedroom almost identical except two different girls. All four were, I guessed, of

Mediterranean or Slavic origin--Lebanon, Turkey, Spain--dark hair, olive skin, oval shape faces, pretty--in a dead sort of way. I estimated three days tops. Their faces had begun to change, as is the progression of death. They had all died within a small window of time. I walked back into the hall.

"Where's the Thune's bedroom, Gumshoe? It must be off the kitchen."

But no, the door from kitchen only led to the garage, and it was empty except for a green Mazda sporty number. We had only two minutes before Hector would unleash the dogs, so it was back to the hallway going to the front of the house.

The main room in front, in addition to the usual furnishings was filled with cardboard boxes. A locked door prevented us from entering another room off to one side. I assumed it was the main bedroom, and hoped it would reveal something of value for our purposes.

"Open some boxes--a couple or three randomly, Fox, and take pictures of contents. I'm going to open that door, one way or another."

"I have a screwdriver out . . ."

"Out in the garden. Yes, thanks, Fox," I chortled. "I'll use a bit more finesse."

I slammed my shoulder into the door, splintering it. Stepping through, I saw a large, very tidy room, two dressers, queen bed with no bodies, and several framed pictures--including, I assumed, family portraits. Without examining them I took photos of all.

There were two other doors off the bedroom, one I assumed was a bathroom, the other a closet.

"Gumshoe, we need to roll. We're a minute over already."

I flipped a coin, and examined the closet. One side of the racks was loaded with uniforms--all different branches of service, as well as police; the other side in female uniforms--from nurses to military.

On a shelf my eye spotted two binders and a box the size of a greeting card box. I started to open one of the binders when Fox whistled.

"Gumshoe, I said we need to roll. We're already way over." Quick decision: take it all . . . examine later.

* * *

We were just parking in front of our unit when we heard the sirens. Hector gave an excuse for a wave as he passed. Other official vehicles passed as well.

"I liked your 'little more finesse', Gumshoe," Fox giggled, as she loaded her usb cable to her camera.

"We were running behind. I could have used my lock-picking tools or a kitchen knife."

"Don't forget one of my bobby pins."

"Of course, one of your bobby pins. Do you have any?"

"No."

"See? That would have taken much longer."

"Okay, Gumshoe," Fox grew serious, "here are the pictures of the boxes. I opened two. Crammed with clothing, mostly lingerie, as you can see. I'm thinking advertising props for porn? So where's your camera?"

Fox cringed as she looked at the four dead females. She agreed they were at one time striking beauties with similar characteristics.

"You really think European, Gumshoe?"

"Perhaps Mediterranean, Middle East, yes. By the way, don't upload anything to the hard drive; keep it all on the cameras. The next group of pictures I took was in the Thune bedroom, probably family . . . I didn't even look at them; I simply snapped pictures."

"So, let's see what you thought was important enough to snap."

Thune and three other men--brothers? . . . Thune and woman--wife? . . . Thune and same woman--plus another of Thune with same woman and older couple--mother and father? . . . two or three more of same. One especially intriguing: Thune and same woman in Coast Guard garb, both officers.

"Gumshoe!" Fox exclaimed.

"That's it for pictures, Fox," I said.

"Gumshoe, listen to me!" she almost shouted. "Look at this picture!"

It was of Thune and the female dressed in Coast Guard garb.

"We've met her, Gumshoe. that's that procurement woman on the yacht! That Louisa! She came back with Henry in the Cutter!"

I studied the computer screen. "Son of a gun! You're right! Henry thought she was vaguely familiar! She must have been here in Key West at one time or another."

"But she's not Thune's wife. Let's find out who she is, Bossman."

"Later. Right now I think a drink would be about right."

"See? I told you I love you. You have the uncanny ability to prioritize. I'll join you."

I poured two fingers of Martell for Fox, a like amount for myself, and reached for the binders, handing one of them to Fox.

"These binders could be holding nothing of importance," I shrugged, "I grabbed them because you hurried me."

"Yeah, yeah," Fox chided as she opened to the first page. It was in the form of a loose-leaf ledger --forty lines, eight columns, but only five used, dating back to 2013. She thumbed through a few of the sixty-plus pages. On the reverse side of each page were hand-written notes in script. The binder was chock full through December of 2017.

"It looks like a page for each month, Bossman."

"Yes," I said, as I opened my binder. "Ahhh, mine is a continuation . . . beginning January, 2018."

I flipped to the last page of writing . . . "and the last entry is the month of October. Makes sense.

Hmmm, Looks like some kind of P. and L. ledger. Yours is the same right?"

"Yeah, money going in and out, but no bank information, Bossman."

The pages had a 'date', a 'description', an 'out' an 'in', and then a 'totals' line in the eighth column at the bottom right. October was almost decipherable

Day	Description	out	in	Bank
1st	-- Bet (H)	-- Ø	-- $150K	
2nd	-- Ø			

3rd   -- Fee advance (H)   -- \$20k   --   Ø

I turned the page and began to read to her:
1st-- won bet. said I would. Ha!

I reached for the Martell. "What do you make of that, Fox?"

"A lot of money on a bet, Gumshoe. Maybe for scuttling the *Blue Moon?*" She held her glass out; I topped it off.

The Blue Moon? That's what I thought, too. Who would make such a wager with a dirty cop? I took another two fingers of Martell as well. *Something to ponder, Gumshoe. Another dirty cop?*

I continued reading. Fox reached for her binder when I whistled.

"Fox! Listen to this! It's the next entry, in fact the last one on the back side of October. It's short, but it's about you."

Fox lay her binder aside, took a sip of cognac and waited, her eyes fixed on me.

October
3rd--bitch is alive. belongs to P.I. must eliminate both-- especially her. H -\$80K contract -- 20K advance

"That's about you as well, Gumshoe, not just me!

Just thumbing through this binder," she held hers up, "Thune always uses initials in his entries. *H* figures in quite a few of them almost from the very first month back in 2013. Listen to this from

September:

Day	Description	out	in	Bank
14th -- 22 units (Mx)	--	44K(H)	-- \$220K	

"Then on the reverse side of September he writes:

September
  14th -- easy $$$ --176K - **H** big help - good addition

"I don't know if he's trafficking or pushing drugs or what, but he certainly finds it lucrative."

"He does indeed. *H* receives a fee, Thune ends up with a real chunk of change . . . and this goes back to 2013? Wow! He has a stash somewhere."

"Both of them do, Gumshoe. So, who is *H*?"

"I don't know; could be anyone." I pushed my fedora back and rubbed my eyes, "Hector? Henry? Noooo!" I shook my head, "Can't be one of them."

But Fox countered, "From where I sit, Gumshoe, no one is off limits."

"Oh, hell . . . may as well start with Henry," I sighed. "Bring that ledger and your laptop."

43

Thursday, Oct 17
2:30 p.m.
Who is "H"

Ensign Brady smiled. "You two again? Lieutenant Commander Martaise is in with him. You can wait in the garden, I'll let him know you're here."

"I hate to even ask Henry the tough questions about any involvement, but I intend to open that binder and let him have a gander. Pay attention to his face as I show him."

Henry apologized as he came into the garden a few minutes later.

"Quite a discovery, Garrett! Four young women. My goodness."

"Did you enter the house, Henry?"

"Oh, no. Police business, but Hector called me to confirm everything you said was true. You certainly have a knack for finding problems my friend."

"Not finding problems, Henry. Uncovering creeping crud."

"More like an infection going on for . . . who knows how long. A dirty cop, dirty guardsman, dirty harbor master and assistant. Who else will come up dirty, Garrett?"

"Not sure, Henry, but there are possibly, even probably, more. I have something to show you, and I'd like your opinion."

"Sure. What'cha got for me?"

Fox handed Henry the more current ledger. "We retrieved this from Thune's home this morning. Please look through it, Mr. Waite," she said, "especially the October page of this year."

"Sure." Henry thumbed through several pages, whistling several times at the extraordinary amounts of money coming into the Thune coffers. He then noted verbally many of the several times *"H"* was involved in the exchanging of money, and the obvious 'assassin' assignment given him by the ledger's author, obviously Gary Thune.

"And you're showing me this because? . . ."

"You're not *H* are you Henry?" I asked the question point blank. I didn't beat around the bush.

"Wow!" Henry drew in a breath. "That hurts, Garrett!" he responded, slowly shaking his head. "I'm not sure you're welcome here anymore." He shoved the ledger forcefully into my ribcage.

"Either one of you! I'll have Ensign Brady show you out for the last time. Do your investigating somewhere else." He turned on his military heel and departed.

"That went well, Bossman," Fox said, looking at me. "Too brusque?"

"Yeah, tactless . . . but, did you notice, he didn't answer my question."

Ensign Brady came rushing into the garden. "What did you say to the Commander? He's really pissed! I'm told to escort you out of our office with no return invite."

"We understand, Ensign. We're looking for a bad guy with an initial 'H', and in a dismissive gesture Garrett, here, asked the Commander if he was perhaps the 'H' of our search."

"Oh, cripe!" Brady sighed, "there are a few 'H's' in Key West! . . . but that shouldn't bend his nose out of shape. We'd better get you out of here before I get a chewing out."

"If you think of someone, we'd appreciate a name," Fox told her, giving her a card.

"Of course."

And with that we were ushered out.

* * *

"Hector?"

"Yeah, may as well have our asses kicked to the door twice in one day . . . get it over with."

We swung by the liquor store, picked up a bag of salted peanuts and a bottle of Martell and headed for the Key West Police Precinct.

We parked and went inside. Monte Mońez was at the desk.

"Go on in. He's expecting you," Monte said and nodded his head toward the corridor leading to Hector's office. "Fair warning, though, he's in a mood."

"Henry called?" Fox asked.

"Yes, but . . ."

"Enough said, Monte," Fox laughed. I held her hand as as she turned around to face him, walking backwards, waving the bottle of Martell . . . We continued down the hallway, definitely in for an ass-chewing.

Hector looked up as we knocked on his open door.

"Well, well!" he roared. "The two snoop-dogs! And how appropriate! One has his nuts bottled and in his hand!"

He stood and roared with laughter, shook our hands, then motioned for us to sit. I set the peanuts on his desk.

"You really upset Henry, you know, but Henry's not in the world of day to day police work. Hell, I'd question my own grandmother if her name was Henrietta."

He retrieved three glasses and a bowl, poured out three generous slugs of Martell and motioned to the bowl.

"Now Garrett, let's try your . . ."

"Hector, stop! Vulgarity doesn't suit you!" Fox exclaimed. "I'd like to remember you as a true gentleman when I write my memoirs."

"I am a true gentleman! But I take your point, Miss. No more ribald humor! Now let's take a look at that book you took from the Thune house."

"Two books, Hector. Going back to 2013, but before we get to that, what else did you find in that house in addition to four dead women?"

"My people are still going through it. We found a crawlspace in the ceiling of the garage with a stack of cocaine bricks worth millions and behind an air vent in the master bedroom wall was a string of plastic-wrapped bundles of cash.

Tim pulled on one package and tied with a string was another, then another . . . kept going for nine or ten packages . . . and that's just for starters. We haven't even counted it yet, but we figure two-three million minimum."

"Wow, that's a bunch of bucks!" Fox declared.

Hector received a call. He mumbled something and smiled a broad, phony smile as he hung up.

"Yes," he continued without missing a breath, "and there may be more. As I said, we're still there, combing through the house inch by inch. Now about the ledgers."

"You may as well keep them," Fox said, handing both ledgers to Hector. "We're done with them, right, Bossman?"

"Yeah, we've seen enough to get the idea. It's a seven year diary of corruption. Our only concern at present is the identity of "H". I had already scratched Henry and you, but we had to cross every 't' and dot every 'i', you understand."

"Absolutely," Hector nodded as he reached for the ledgers . . . a bit too anxious, I thought. I frowned. Hector took note and smiled.

"What now, Gumshoe? I reached a bit too fast? You are good. No, actually I want the ledgers put away before the FBI team walks in the door.

That was Monte on the horn. He let me know they've just parked their car in our lot. They'll be here in a minute."

I said the only thing I could think of . . .

"Shit!"

44

Thursday, Oct 17
4:50 p.m.,
Burgundy Mercedes

"By all means, send them in, Monte."

The trio marched in without so much as a "how-do-you-do", and looked around for chairs. Hector and I stood with outstretched hands as gentlemen; Fox remained seated.

"Monte!" Hector yelled down the hallway, "find us a few more chairs for our guests, please."

"No worries, Chief," I shrugged, "we were just leaving, anyway."

"No! Stay, Mr. Garrett," the FBI team leader stated with an inflated sense of authority. "You seem to be involved in every aspect of Key West crime anyway. I have a few things to tell the Chief, then some questions for you. Stick around!"

"Hmph." I frowned, "not sure that's a compliment or a slap in the face, but just for fun we'll stay."

"Quite a build-up, Miss." Hector said as Monte brought three folding chairs in.

"Wait! Wait!" Fox said. "Hector, you have a conference room, much more appropriate for a crowd of six. I suggest we move."

"I was about to recommend the same, my good lady," and with that he led the way into the police lunch room. Of course, I brought our bottle.

Fox opened a cupboard, pulled out six glasses and set them before each of us. Then she poured. One of the FBI fellows turned his glass upside down; the others thanked her.

Hector raised his glass, "Here's to the swift conclusion of the pervasive criminal influence here in Key West."

Everyone joined him in a sober toast.

He then turned to the FBI leader. "The floor is yours, Ma'am."

Miss Hughes took a mouthful of Martell Cognac and smiled wryly.

"Yesterday we were told of Gary Thune's burgundy Mercedes. It theoretically pulled into Thune's driveway at approximately 7:30 a.m., backed out of the driveway and continued in the same direction. Why would Mr. Thune do that? To pick up someone? Let's leave that for the moment.

My team went down the road this morning, you thought, on a wild goose chase to this remote spot called *Old Finds Bight* while you were searching Thune's house.

I don't know what you found, but, 'surprise, surprise!' we found the Mercedes! It was parked in a gravel parking lot at the end of a muddy dirt road. The only reason we found it is the fresh tire tracks."

"Did you get to the water?" Fox asked.

"No! The road ended at the parking lot," she laughed. "From there the Mercedes occupants-- and there were three or four, minimum--must have transferred to a second, waiting vehicle."

"How can you be sure of that?" Fox asked . . . "it was graveled you said."

"Reading and following shoe and tire tracks," she answered, with irritation. "The gravel was thin enough to expose the dirt and get good impressions."

It was like brushing a pesky mosquito away. She drained her Martell, waved off a second pour, and continued. "I'm having the Mercedes towed in for examination later today. We should capture some good fingerprints."

"Unless they wiped it down," I observed, "but good for your team. As I understand it, however, there is a hidden trail from the parking lot going all the way to a barge sitting on the water. Too bad you didn't find that trail.

If that's it, Fox and I will be going. We'll be at our motel room after dinner. Good day, gentlemen, Ma'am."

As we made our way to the motel, Fox smiled, "Did that 'trail' remark have a purpose, Bossman?"

"You think it irritated her a little bit?" I gave her a sidelong look. We both laughed.

"The Hungry Pelican?"

"Sounds good, Gumshoe," Fox agreed. "I feel like a good ol' cheeseburger and fries."

"And perhaps some time to breathe," I added.

It was not to be.

45

Thursday, Oct 17
5:30 p.m.
So much for peace and quiet

Our friend Jennifer and her brother, Marvin, or Munch as I recalled his nickname, were sitting in a booth at the restaurant. They were just finishing their dinners and drinks. Spying us, the two welcomed us to join them.

"So much for peace and quiet," Fox mumbled, but we smiled and scooted in beside them.

"So, how do you like your new employment, Jennifer?" I asked as the waiter came by, took our cheeseburger orders from Fox.

"Oh, Mr. Garrett, it is the best!" she said enthusiastically. "My instructor, Francisco Bardos says I'll be ready to be on my own by January. School semester is over then, and I'm told my grades are at the top."

"You're actually going to be put out there on your own?" With a look of shock, I furrowed my brow.

"Yup."

"Days or nights?"

"Days, just like now."

"Who's on night duty?"

No one has been assigned yet, but word is it will be Francisco."

"So it's not manned right now?"

"Not for over a week."

"A major port of entry?" I shook my head. "Not good."

"There's not much happening, though; no craft coming in our going out that I have seen in my two days on the job."

That produced a hearty laugh from all of us.

"Give it a month on the job, Jen," warned Marvin, "you'll be changing your mind about how easy it is."

"No, I won't! I am determined to be a great Harbor Master; I'm not afraid of hard work."

"Good for you, Jen," Fox tipped her glass toward the young lady. "Stand tall."

Our burgers came. Jen reached for a fry off my plate, then she and Munch rose to go as I was complaining about her theft. I cut my burger in two and started to take a bite. But not Fox.

"Wait! Wait, Jen. I do have a question for you, before you go. We know Gary Thune's wife owns a Medline zodiac in a slip in the harbor. Has it traveled in or out of the harbor to your knowledge? It's in slip # . . . uh," Fox reached into her purse and drew out a listing of the Medlines. "Ahhh, slip #301. That's the third slip on the left as you walk down the main pier."

"Yes, I'm familiar with the zodiac. I didn't realize it belonged to Thune. It was there Sunday. I remember it well, because it's such a nice craft. It was not there Tuesday morning about 9:30 but it was there at noon. Today it was missing all day. That I can say for sure."

"Folks," Marvin said, taking Jen's arm, "I'm on duty tonight. Have a good evening. Come on, Squeaky." With that, they left us.

* * *

"Good information, Fox," I said approvingly.

"Why, thanks, Gumshoe."

We were just finishing our dinner when Henry walked in.

Fox saw him first. Her jaw dropped, "You must be kidding Gumshoe. Do we leave a trail of crumbs for people to find us?"

He came directly to our table and seated himself without invite.

"Good evening. First of all, I apologize for the way I acted earlier. I was out of line. You are welcome to come into my house whenever."

"Thank you, Henry, and you're welcome to our table any time as well."

"Provided you pick up the check," Fox added, smiling.

"Happy to," Henry pulled a credit card out of a shirt pocket. We didn't stop him. It was, after all, only $17.44.

"I'm here--in addition to apologizing--to pass along a situation that has just come to my attention.

I attended the funerals, Tuesday, right? Lieutenant Commander Martaise was given the assignment of delivering the two female prisoners to the Monroe County Detention Center here in Key West.

From there they were to go by bus to the ICE Detention center in Miramar. I called the center to make the arrangements myself. Miramar called this evening, asking when to expect them. I don't know where they went, but it appears they didn't go to Miramar, Garrett."

"Interesting, Henry. What did Martaise say about it?"

"That's the strange thing. She was in my office this morning, I believe you came in at the time-- you may have seen her. She had to scoot out the door to go home. Her mother was involved in a hit and run and is in a hospital in Missouri."

"So she's not here to defend herself," Fox noted.

"Not just that," Henry noted, "but something doesn't smell right. I really don't know the woman. She comes with a great dossier: been with the Guard for twelve years, several posts--from Texas to North Carolina."

"What are you suggesting, Henry?" I asked.

"I'm suggesting she may have ulterior motives. I'm suggesting she may be in league with Officer Gary Thune."

"You're suggesting she may have spirited away those two prisoners Tuesday, aren't you?" Fox raised an eyebrow.

"I'm afraid she may be your 'H'," Henry warned. "Her name is Helen, remember."

"Yes, I know. I was going to ask your opinion of her this morning, but . . ." I shrugged my shoulders . . . "You realize, Henry," I continued, "she would need some influential pull to receive the Key West posting. If I were you, I'd research her background, all the way back to college, high school, even. See if there's a link to Thune. Or, alternatively, see who put her down here, next to him."

"But don't forget Missouri," Fox cautioned. "She could be on the up and up. Call that number first."

"Thanks, I will. In fact it's early in Missouri. I'll call this evening. I'll let you know."

"What do you think, Bossman?" Fox asked, once Henry was gone.

"I think I need a drink," I replied. "Let's go home. I mean to Room 47."

46

Thursday, Oct 17
7:00 p.m.
The call from Hector

Fox and I were just walking through the motel room door when my cell phone rang. "That kid you've been looking for, Gumshoe, I think . . ."

"Wait a second, Hector," I interrupted, "let me put my packages down," I gave Fox a shrug and a hopeful look, set a couple of bags of junk food down and grabbed a glass. "Okay, Hector, what about the kid?"

"I think he was being held in the Thune house. His prints are in several places, so I don't know if it was against his will or not, but I think so. Why do I think so, you ask? Because he slept in the bathtub, and there were chains on the bathroom wall."

"You're kidding, Hector!" Fox exploded."You didn't see that?" Hector laughed, shaking his head.

"Damn, Gumshoe, I thought you were a private investigator!"

"You gave us five minutes . . . I didn't get to the

bathroom. Fox kept yelling at me."

"There's more."

"There's more? Isn't that enough?" I asked. "Give me a minute to take my shoes off, pour a cognac and get comfortable," I said. "It's been a long day already."

Fox brought us each a Martell, proceeded to take my shoes off, then sat in my lap and adjusted herself as Hector waited on speaker. He finally said, "Are you two okay over there?"

"Yes, fine. I just had an elbow push a rib into my backbone is all," I winced, and took a sip. Fox only grinned.

Hector continued on speaker. "Thune's red Mercedes is in my yard. FBI crew is ripping it apart as we speak. They shared their first findings with Henry and me. Fingerprints.

Helen Martaise, the two females, Claudia and Louisa--the two she was supposed to take to the Sheriff, and your boy, Paul Maggorie."

"And Thune?" Fox asked.

"We have prints, but they're not within the last five days," Hector said.

"What? You can tell how old a print is?" Fox was dumbfounded.

"Yes," I broke in. "New CSI technology in 2014 and 2015. Not yet perfected, but proven accurate within five days, and if within 3 days we can pinpoint it to within an hour. A sweat and body oils thing."

I took another sip of cognac, and whispered to Fox to move a bit more to the right so she wouldn't break my leg. She moved a bit. In pain I tried to muffle a euphemism.

"Is that really true, Gumshoe, about the fingerprints?"

Hector laughed, "You two have obviously stopped paying attention to me. I'll hang up now."

"Not yet, please. What are your thoughts, Hector?"

"Henry says a zodiac picked them up. I'll go with that."

"I think so, too. I figure Thune himself was waiting at *Oyster Cove* for his crew and the boy."

"What about Helen Martaise?" I wondered "She was in Henry's office this morning. Talk about a woman with ice in her veins."

"Well, young man, you have a contract on your head, you know . . . and don't forget who has the chore of filling it, and receiving the reward. Of course, there's ice in her veins. Sleep with your .45, Garrett." We hung up.

"Son of a bitch, Fox! He was right here in Key West! And we missed him!" I gently scooted Fox off my lap so I could rant properly.

"Not your fault, Gumshoe," she consoled me as I paced the floor. "Who knows when he was brought back. Remember they've had no harbor master for the past week or so."

"I suppose you're right, Liz, I guess we just chalk it up to one missed opportunity and move on. I need to call the general, though."

General Maggorie interrupted me as soon as I said my 'hello'.

"Garrett, that's impeccable timing! I just returned home after three days away, opened my stack of mail, and you know what I found? I found a frigging ransom letter!"

"When, Sir?"

"Shut up and listen, dammit! A million bucks! That's what they want! One million dollars!"

"Post-marked when and where, Sir?"

"Miami, and . . . uh, looks like, uh, Monday. Yes, postmarked Monday from Miami. But one million dollars, Garrett! One million!"

"How are you supposed to contact him?"

"A numbered account in some Atlantic bank in Belize by today. Hell, Garrett, I just returned home this evening."

Remembering some contacts from my last case, I said, "Give me the account number, Sir. I have friends in Belize banking—specifically, the Atlantic International Bank, as well as a top federal policeman, a Jose Gallo."

"That's the bank, Garrett," he said as he read off the number. "But what can you do?"

"I don't know yet, but I'll call them tomorrow morning and see if there's anything helpful. In the meantime, here's my news: Paul was being held in Key West just yesterday. If things go well, we'll rescue him within forty-eight hours."

"You've said that before, Garrett!"

"I didn't know Liz and I are dealing with such corruption. These aren't petty criminals, Sir. Members of the police, coast guard and European organized crime are involved. We've really stirred up a hornet's nest."

"Call me tomorrow morning, Garrett." The phone went dead.

The rest of the evening we spent watching a few crime dramas on TV while enjoying a couple of beers and munching microwaved popcorn.

At 10 p.m. Fox thumbed through the three major media outlets for news . . . finding only biased diatribe. *(Whatever happened to David Brinkley, John Cameron Swayze or Walter Cronkite . . . real newsmen?)*

She tossed me the remote and announced, "Time for a shower."

She disappeared for twenty minutes. I flipped to an episode of Gunsmoke. Fox returned, looking lovely, dressed in a motel robe and smelling of something akin to apples.

I took my turn showering. Coming out, I found her feigning sleep in the bed next to my fedora. The robe was across the room on the other king-size bed.

"Scoot over," I ordered.

"No," she answered.

It was dark. I carefully folded my boxer shorts, lay them on the nightstand, set my .45 on top. Now I had a decision to make: *are you going to drag her beautiful bottom out of bed, guide her to the other one, Gumshoe?*

While I was contemplating, Fox pulled back the linen and reached out. It was dark, but not that dark. Easy decision.

"Umm, you smell delicious."

"Ummmm, you may nibble if you like, Gumshoe."

47

Friday, Oct 18
6:15 a.m.
A New Day

"Yes, please," I smiled up at Marge as she came around with the carafe. Fox nodded and held her mug out for Marge as well.

"You two look like you're still half asleep," Marge laughed as she took our orders. "Coffee should perk you right up."

"Just leave the carafe, Marge," Fox smiled back; "we'll need a second, and then a third cup."

"Can't do that, but I'll be back," she assured us.

"Before you go, Marge, how well do you know Beverley Thune?"

"Bunny? I guess, as well as anyone. She was not very neighborly, away quite often, haven't seen her since around the first of October."

I showed her the pictures I had taken in the Thune bedroom.

"Thune is in these pictures with different women...which one is Bunny?"

She pointed to the picture of Thune and a woman, both dressed as Coast Guardsmen.

"This one is Bunny, but this one," she pointed to a picture of Thune with another woman, dressed in Coast Guard garb, "I'm pretty sure this is Thune's sister. I met her a little over a year ago as they were entering his house. She wasn't wearing a police uniform, though. They must play 'dress-up' a lot. Strange!" She laughed and went about her business.

"Now we know which one is Mrs. Thune," I smiled.

"Right. She's the one in the Coast Guard."

While awaiting our food I called Jose Gallo in Belize.

"Jose, remember me, the investigator from California? . . . and a good day to you as well . . ." I explained I was looking for a criminal with a numbered bank account, possibly at the Atlantic International Bank in San Ignacio or Belize City. I gave him the account number and asked if he could help locate the account and the branch.

"As soon as the bank opens, I'll call Natalia Duran, the bank manager."

"Si, Señor. I'm sure we will find the number for you," Jose said. Then came, "Señor Garrett, it is only 5:30 in the morning here. It is very early."

"Oh, I'm sorry, Jose." I stumbled over myself trying to apologize. "I thought it was 7:30 a.m. I won't call you this early again." I hung up and looked sheepishly at Fox. "Nuts! I knew it was an hour different. I went the wrong way."

She yawned and smiled. "Awake now? We should probably go back to our room and catch up on our sleep. Just a suggestion, Sweetie."

I raised an eyebrow as I looked at her. "Funny lady."

Breakfast came, as did more coffee and a half dozen of the Key West old-timers. They joined in rowdy praise for cleaning up the police department, the coast guard, the harbor authority, and any number of other things, including the town dog catcher.

Didn't matter that they had every fact stretched out of proportion and upside down; what mattered was that it involved no politics--it was simply misplaced heroism; we were fighting corruption in their town . . . therefore, we were heroes. One of them even said it was too bad I didn't show up in time to save *The Blue Moon*.

Fox and I downplayed our contribution, only that we were privileged to be part of the team along with Hector and Henry and their respective forces, plus two of their own--Ernie and Sam, who figured mightily.

Two cups of coffee later I looked at the time. "It's 7:30, Fox. I wond . . . "

"6:30 in Belize," she interrupted.

"Yes, thanks. I wonder if Henry is in." I made the call. Fox leaned into my shoulder so we could both hear.

Our gang of old-timers withdrew to a large table in the middle of floor as more of their cronies walked in.

Fox laughed, "They could probably solve all the world's problems, given a couple of hours."

"And a tape recorder to remember what they said," I added.

"Oooops, here's Henry . . . good morning, Henry. Is there any news on a possible Missouri connection?"

"Well, she checked in at the airport in Miami, for a St. Louis flight, Garrett, but the record shows she didn't board."

"Okay, thanks Henry. I'll alert Hector."

"Already did. Watch yourself. You have a contract on your head--actually both of you."

"Yeah, we know. Thanks. We have some news for you as well, Henry. Looks like your gal, Helen Martaise could be Gary Thune's sister. Introduced to Marge as such."

"Marge at the *Pelican*?"

"Yes."

"Twelve years in the Guard, Garrett. I wonder when she turned?"

"Ledgers tell us at least six years, Henry."

"Looks like they're pulling up stakes," Fox commented. "Too hot here," she added.

"Or they're retiring," Henry said.

"People like Thune don't retire easily, Henry, they become obsessed with the game, the power and the thrill. But," I added with a smile, "I think retirement will be swift and final for our Mr. Thune. And," I added, "I'd like to assist."

"You and three or four others, Garrett. Good hunting. I need to go, my new harbor master just walked in."

"Jennifer? I asked.

"Yes." He chuckled as he hung up.

Marge came by. "Fresh coffee? I'll dump the old."

"Yes, that would be great, thanks."

So as we were enjoying a fresh, fourth cup my phone rang again.

"Garrett, it's Henry again. If you remember, I told you I put a tracker on Thune's boat. It's gone. The boat's gone! Jennifer just confirmed that she noticed it missing between 3:30 and 4 p.m. I didn't notice it. She just walked the marina pier and it's still gone, as is Mrs. Thune's zodiac. I have a fix on its location. Do you want a ride?"

"Absolutely! We'll be there." I almost shouted. "Give us fifteen minutes."

"It will take me a half hour to get a boat prepared. Take your time. Figure on meeting me here at 9:30 a.m."

Fox broke in, "Wait, Bossman, did you forget Belize?"

"Oh! Yes, I did forget, thanks. Henry, I have a couple of phone calls to make, but I can't make them until 10 a.m. How about 11:00 a.m.?"

"Fine. I have other things to do anyway. See you at 11."

Fox winked, "We could go back to the motel and . . . you know," she batted her eyes at me.

"Stop right there, Fox," I laughed, shaking my head. "We have work to do."

"We have two hours, Gumshoe. What do you suggest? More coffee?"

"Let's take a walk on the pier. It's a warm, bright morning."

"You take your walk; I'm going back to our room. I need to use the 'ladies' and maybe catch up on a bit of sleep." She stood, blew me a kiss and walked out.

* * *

I sat at Ginny's kiosk feeding the birds, considering the last evening and smiling broadly. *Is this a partner you've been waiting for, Alan? Not just as your business partner but as your life partner? She is certainly impressive in so many ways; she's sharp, witty, clear-headed, catches on easily, and . . . did I mention exuberant? Wow is she ever!* My smile widened even more.

I was almost out of apple fritter. The birds were getting restless. A couple of them even hopped up on the bench beside me to get their fair share. I asked their opinion on my thoughts of the morning.

One grabbed a piece of fillo pastry and flew off, but the other cocked her head and listened intently to my thoughts before taking a bite (I determined at that point it was female) then took the last bite from my fingers, looked at me for a moment more then flew off. At least she listened.

I started back, armed with an apple fritter for Fox, but who should I meet but Jennifer, preparing for her morning duties.

"Where's your Guardsman teacher, what's his name . . . Francisco?"

"Bardos," she smiled. I meet him here every morning. I'm a bit early. Did you notice, there's a boat in Thune's boat slip?"

"No! I didn't go out on that pier. What slip is it?"

She walked me out to where Gary Thune's boat was up until yesterday . . . when Jennifer had told Henry it was missing, sometime after 3 p.m.

Now, in it's place, was a sleek jet-ski boat, similar to the one we had chased near Dominica.

"That worries me, Jennifer. I need to go." I trotted down the pier toward the street, then I turned back.

"Don't let that boat leave the harbor!" I yelled, then continued toward the street, leaving her wondering what was so worrying.

She would know before the day ended. I picked up the pace as I hit the street.

48

Friday, Oct 18
9:45 a.m.
More than a friend

An ambulance and two police cars were in front of the motel as I rushed up the block. I could see the ambulance crew discussing something with Hector as yet another ambulance pulled into the driveway.

"Hector!" I called out. "What's happened?"

Hector tapped on the ambulance rear door. It sped away.

"Your lady friend is what's happened," Hector said, as I caught up with him. "I'm afraid she tangled with that assassin lady, *H,* and it didn't turn out very well . . . for either of them, actually."

"How is she? Where is she?"

"How? I'm not sure Garrett; where? on her way to the hospital in that rig," he said pointing at the tail-lights heading toward the hospital.

"You saw me!" I exploded. "Why didn't you tell them to wait so I could talk to her?"

"Because, Asshole!" he bellowed right back, "I didn't want her to bleed out on the floor while we wait for you!"

My jaw dropped. I had no words.

"Now," he said calmly, "settle down for a moment . . . hop into my squad car. We'll ride to the hospital together, and I'll bring you up to date on what I know. You would not have been able to talk with her right now anyway."

"Is she badly hurt, Hector?"

"Let's wait to make our determination, Garrett. There were two wounded in the room, blood everywhere; guests in neighboring units gave conflicting reports. One woman said she heard eight shots, another fellow said many more--at least fifteen.

Surprisingly, fifteen sounds more logical. Your lady's Beretta has only five rounds remaining in her magazine, so she could have used ten, herself. That's a nice gun, by the way. Haven't seen one before."

"The latest Beretta-92. A few new innovations," I replied. Hector continued, "So that's ten shots. The assassin had a .22 with suppressor--an eight round Beretta-71--their favorite for wet work. Only two rounds left. Bullets were flying everywhere, Garrett. I brought in two ambulances because, frankly, I still don't know the status of either woman. My guys will give me a report on 'H'.

Now let's go check on your lady."

"Thanks, Hector," I sighed a long sigh. "Sounds like she did what she could. She'd better still be alive; I swear, Chief, I'll kick her butt all the way back to Manhattan Beach if she dies on me!"

"You sound like you're more than just her boss, my friend," Hector gave me a wistful smile.

"I'm trying to figure that out, Hector," I said as we pulled into the 'police parking only' spot at the hospital. I slid out of the police cruiser.

"Let's hope for the best," he said as we rushed up the steps to the emergency entrance.

A nurse I remembered smiled at us.

"Hello, Chief, and hello again, Mr. Garrett. Remember me? I'm Jackie. And we have your lady again, don't we?

She's just gone into surgery, gentlemen. I'm sorry I can't tell you more, except, as you know, she suffered multiple gunshot wounds. She has a strong heartbeat, Mr. Garrett. Be optimistic."

"How soon can I see her?" I asked.

"Give me your card. I'll call you." She studied the card for a moment--"oh, yes. *Gumshoe and Fox*. I'll call as soon as I have word from upstairs, Mr. Gumshoe."

"And the other one?" Hector asked.

"We were expecting one more female, but the driver canceled a minute before you walked in. She's being transported to the morgue."

"Thanks. Do call me," I said. We walked out.

As we hopped back into his cruiser, Hector said, "The wicked witch is dead, Garrett. No more looking over your shoulder."

"I just wish it had been me in that room, Hector, that's all."

"Where to, Garrett, motel or morgue?" Hector asked.

"Don't even say that, Hector . . . drop me off at the motel before you head for the morgue."

"Sorry, Garrett. Not thinking. Motel it is."

Henry called while I was exiting the cop car.

"Garrett, I heard you've had a disaster. How is Fox?"

"Hard to say. She's still in the operating room."

"Do you want to hold off on our hunt?"

"No, I'm more determined than ever, Henry. I want to visit the hospital as soon as Jackie calls me, then I'll be ready. Hang on a minute, Henry."

I poked my head inside my motel room. It would certainly require an industrial cleanup, complete with a new paint job. I shook my head.

"Sorry, I just looked inside my motel room, Henry, but back to business -- Thune has a jet boat in his slip. It was used by Helen Martaise sometime late yesterday or early this morning to sneak back to Key West to kill Fox and me. He's expecting her to ret ..."

"I see where you're going, Garrett. You want to use his jet boat to catch up with him."

"Yes I do, Henry. It's the best way to get close enough."

"I'll go with you," Henry said.

"No. I'm thinking there can be only one in that boat. But," I continued, "I'd like you and Hector to follow me at a distance."

"Okay," Henry said. "I'll call Hector to see if he has some time. Thune's boat is about two hours away. It's just sitting in the water and now I see why ... Thune is waiting for his half-sister."

"She's a half-sister?"

"Yeah, if that. We did some more digging. They were banged around in several foster homes in Missouri. It looks like she joined him in the last home, where the father was a super-strict cop."

"Henry," I interrupted, "I need to place a couple of calls. I'll call you when I'm ready to pull out. We'll coordinate."

I called the bank in Belize and was directed to the assistant manager, Natalia Duran.

"Mr. Garrett, I've been expecting your call. Officer Gomez called earlier. The bank in Belize City has the numbered account you're looking for. Of course, I cannot release the ownership to you, you understand, nor can I freeze the funds on only your verbal instructions, but let me give you the manager's name--Manuel Torres--in Belize City. Your own FBI will have to submit the proper paperwork."

I thanked her, we said our goodbyes. My next call was to FBI team leader, Teresa Hughes.

"Miss Hughes," I began, "I have some information for you. Please write down the following: Numbered account #B-55565 7841 14CR7X -- Atlantic International Bank, Belize City, Manuel Torres, Manager."

"This is all very interesting. Why should I write it down?"

"The account belongs to Gary Thune. You need to freeze it immediately."

"Oh, why don't you just fly down there and freeze it yourself?" she said in a rather snarky manner. "While you're playing with offshore accounts my team and I have uncovered a naked body out here at Old Finds Bight."

"Ahhh, that would be Dario," I said, and hung up.

49

Friday, Oct 18
11:05 a.m.
Running Late

I walked into the motel room, picked up Fox's purse for her set of keys, all the while counting down from 9 - 8 - 7 -- 6 -- 5 -- 4 . . . Ms. Hughes called back.

"Mr. Garrett! What do you know about Dar . . ." the call from the hospital came through at that moment. I hung up from the FBI and said, "Yes?" to Jackie.

"Gumshoe?"

"Can I see her?" I asked anxiously.

"Yes. For a few moments only, please."

"I'll be right there."

Jackie met me as before. "She's in Room #411. You've been there before, Mr. Garrett."

"Yes, I have." I punched the elevator button. On the fourth floor I met Nell, the floor 'In charge' nurse.

"Back again, Mr. Garrett. Come with me." She led me to Room #411 at the end of the hall.

"Don't try to be funny. If she laughs she'll regret it. She has been shot four times--arm, hand, thigh and stomach. Fortunately for her, all the shells were through and through. Not an organ hit, not a bone shattered." I nodded. *Thank you, God!*

Fox was awake, propped up on the bed and displaying a broad smile.

"Did I get her, Gumshoe?" she whispered.

"You did. She's in the morgue where she belongs. Now I want you to get some rest. I am going after Gary Thune and our boy, Paul. Henry has a fix on his position. He sent the woman to kill you, now he's sitting in one spot on the water, waiting for her to return."

"I should be going with you, Bossman. Give me an hour to put on my make-up."

"You take an hour to put on make-up? . . ." Nell stopped me before I said my gag line . . . so I finished with "get some sleep. I got this."

I kissed her forehead, walked out with Nell, thanked her, placed my fedora back on my head and called Henry.

"I'm ready."

* * *

A Coast Guard Response boat was idling beside Thune's jet boat as I approached the slip. Henry was at the controls. Beside him was Hector. A guardsman was at a gun mount in the aft of the boat.

Jennifer was standing on the wooden pier holding a bowline.

"You're going to need this," Hector said, holding up a single key. "My guys fished it out of the shooter's pocket."

"Oh! Good thinking. Thanks!" I said.

We coordinated exactly how we would intercept our target boat, a forty-four foot *Aquila 44*. It wouldn't be easy. Thune's boat had speeds in excess of 45mph, while the Jet boat could reach about 50mph without flipping, and the Response boat maxes out at about 40mph.

We determined a course line, and vectored a running fix on Thune's boat. It was only one hundred twenty miles out. We should make contact by mid-afternoon. We headed out.

50

Friday, Oct 18
11:35 a.m.
Jet Boat Ride

The sea was calm, the weather quite warm. I opened up the throttle; the jet boat handled beautifully.

Henry had the GPS tracking bug aboard the Coast Guard response boat, so as we neared the hundred mile mark, I throttled down to allow him to hone in on our quarry. He took the lead.

Ten minutes later, Hector's voice came over the radio, "There's a boat with a dinghy within sight, about three miles out, due east. Only one. Fit's the description. We'll hang back until you signal."

"Okay," I answered. "I'll push the squawk box twice when I want you."

The jet boat being so low in the water, I couldn't see the boat in question, but I altered course slightly, throttled up the big Honda motors and roared due east toward the *Aquila 44*.

Should I try to board the boat before Gary, Bunny or whomever else discovered I wasn't

Martaise? . . . or should I go in, guns blazing, disable the big engines, then call in Henry and Hector for the inevitable firefight. The craft came into sight. Indeed, it was the *Aquila 44*. I decided on a variation of option one.

I slowed to a crawl and approached from the stern. I picked up my binoculars to take a closer look. They had surely by now seen me . . . I was less than three hundred yards from their perch in the cabin, yet there was no sound of engines coming to life, no commotion or bustle of life in the cabin; all seemed calm. Bunny's zodiac bobbed on its tether alongside.

There were two visible in the *Aquila 44's* cabin, a woman and a gent. They were in uniforms of some kind. I identified Bunny—and I figured the gent was one of Gary Thune's goons. I saw neither Gary nor Paul. *They must be below,* I thought.

It wasn't the smartest thing to use the radio, but I chanced it.

"Bunny and a hired hand are topside. Objective must be below. Come ahead. I'm boarding. Over."

I carried a shotgun and my .45; a knife on my belt. Ready as I'll ever be.

Pulling alongside the forty-four foot yacht, I prepared to board when a man's face appeared almost directly above me. His naval officer's arm extended downward with a handgun attached. In a pure reflex action I jerked the arm toward me, twisting the gun from the hand. It dropped into the water. The man followed. His shoulder cracked against the edge of the jet boat on his way down. He let out a yelp as he went under. He came to the surface sputtering.

I backed the jet boat five feet away from the *Aquila 44*. From there I could see most of the yacht's surface. The fellow in the water tried to regain the yacht deck. I waved a gun at him and told him to stay where he was. He complied.

Now I could see that Bunny and her companion were no longer on the deck; they had obviously gone below; in fact, no one was at the controls.

The response boat was approaching. I brought the jet boat alongside once again. In Spanish, I told the fellow in the water to stay where he was. I pulled the key from the ignition and climbed aboard the yacht. Then I gave the jet boat a push with my foot.

"Get in!" I instructed the swimmer. "Stay there. I'll pick you up later."

Henry and Hector pulled alongside. "What gives, Garrett?" Hector called up at me. "Where is everyone?"

"Ask the Navy Captain back there in the jet boat," I pointed.

Hector and Henry talked between themselves for a couple of minutes. Hector, carrying a canvas bag, joined me on the yacht deck. We discussed the situation in front of us.

In the meantime, Henry called out to us, "There's a total of six on the yacht including two women and a male teenager."

We gave Henry the thumbs up, and finalized our decision.

Hector started, "Gary Thune! Come up topside! Now!"

"You heard him, Gary!" I broke in . . . then in Spanish I continued, "all of you down there, you don't have to die!"

"Bunny!" Hector came back, "get your old man out here! You have one minute!"

No movement or sound came back to us; well over a minute passed. Hector shrugged and looked at me. I nodded On a count he tossed a *flash-bang* into the galley from one side, I tossed a smoke bomb down from the other.

Screams of rage and pain came from below, then up scrambled Bunny Thune, accompanied by two Latinos--a young female dressed in a nurse's uniform--complete with a red cross button, then an older, bearded gent in military garb from, probably Mexico, I thought. *He must be the one sitting with Bunny earlier.* All three were disoriented from the *flash-bang*.

Bunny, herself was in full Coast Guard garb; as she found focus she looked around sheepishly. I grabbed her and pulled her away from the galley opening. The others followed.

"He's crazy!" she said, sobbing, "he's out of control, talking like a lunatic!"

"Bunny, listen to me," I said. "I get that Gary isn't himself right now, but what about the lad down there?"

"He's going to kill him! Without a word of a lie that young boy is as good as dead!"

"What about the fellow still down there with Gary?"

"Rene Terazzo. A bad one. Loyal to Gary to the death!"

One by one we checked the three for weapons. We found none.

"Come here, all three of you," Hector said. "We're going to take you back to Key West. We'll sort everything out once we get home. For right now I want you to swim to the craft right behind me."

The young girl led the way to the edge of the yacht. She dove into the water, bobbed up at the jet boat and climbed aboard. The others followed suit.

"Gary!" Hector called out, "it's over! You have just one minute!"

"You are out of order!" came an outraged voice from the galley below. "What you are doing is unlawful! Our vessel is well beyond U.S. jurisdiction! I will have you behind bars as soon as we return to Florida."

Hector looked at me, shaking his head. Gary Thune was, as Bunny had said, completely insane with deranged infatuation!

"We can hold a trial right here on the deck, Captain Thune!" I shouted, "but you must appear within twenty seconds, otherwise we will have no choice but to disallow your petition."

"Bullshit!" came from below. "I decide any time limits!"

Hector shouted, "5, 4, 3, 2, 1," and tossed another *flash-bang* in the hole. Gary's henchman, Rene Terazzo, bolted up the stairs firing his semi-automatic pistol wildly in every direction.

I took him down with two bullets to his right shoulder as he tried to focus his eyes in the sun. He ended up sitting against a yacht railing, bleeding profusely as his weapon rattled harmlessly, coming to rest at Hector's feet.

Hector left it on the deck and walked to the aft end of the yacht, looked down at the occupants of the jet boat, shaking his head at the variety of uniforms.

The response boat was drifting toward us, almost to the point where fenders were required to keep the two vessels from "kissing" one another. Other than the gentle 'slap' of water on the sides of both boats, all was quiet.

Suddenly from below we heard, in Spanish, a shouted, "Rene? Rene, did you kill the bastards?" more silence . . . "Answer me, Dammit! . . . Who's up there?"

Henry, on board the response boat, became inspired. He cranked up the Coast Guard siren. It blared for 30 seconds or more. Then he went to the bullhorn.

"This is Commander Waite, US Coast Guard!" he stated with authority. "All personnel aboard yacht, show yourselves immediately!"

Great idea, Henry, I thought. I gave Henry a big thumb's up and a smile. But no sounds came from below. I rolled my arms forward in a "more, more, more" gesture, but Henry evidently was fresh out of ideas. I reached out and took the bullhorn.

"You, sir," my voice was a bit lower than Henry's, but I continued with the bullhorn, this time addressing Hector. "You're the Key West Police Chief, right? What is your purpose here on the water?"

Hector boomed out, "Yes, Commander. I'm Chief Hector Rodriguez. I'm here with my team to bring this man, Gary Thune, and his cohorts to justice. He has killed at least ten people in the South Florida Keys. He is, right now, holding for ransom a young man on board below." The Chief could be heard by all, including Thune.

I continued, "You have no jurisdiction here, Chief Rodriguez. You and your men should leave immediately to avoid severe consequences."

Then I turned back to Thune. "You in the galley, if that's true, if you're holding a young man for ransom, you must understand authority and the chain of command, right? Come son, do the right thing!"

There was noticeable shuffling and movement from below, then a head appeared. It was Paul.

Hector reached out his hand and grasped Paul's, then roughly jerked him out of the galley-way as Paul was crying out, "Mr. Garrett!" I handed the megaphone back to Henry and pulled Paul to my side. He gave me a long hug.

Meanwhile, Thune, who had begun his ascent to the top deck, suddenly dropped back down below.

"Garrett?" he screamed. "Is that the Sherlock Holmes from California, the one with the bitch girl Friday? Are you out there, Sherlock? Is your wench with you? Who is out there?"

I took the bullhorn back from Henry. "Gary Thune," I began, "You just couldn't get rid of my lady friend, could you? And you still can't. You tried to drown her, to assassinate her in the hospital, and even today another attempt by your own bitch, Helen.

Oh, by the way, Gary, Helen's guts and blood are spread all over the walls of our motel room. Your forces are dwindling, Gary. Let's see, there was Manny, Ronaldo, Helen, and more, I've forgotten how many, your Belize numbered account has been seized by the FBI, and . . . oh, yes, and your lieutenant, Rene Terazzo is bleeding out on your deck as we speak."

I would have taunted him further, but in an enraged fury, he stormed up the steps, blasting with a 12 gauge pump shotgun as he came.

Including the guardsman manning the deck-mounted gun, four shooters, all from different positions ended his assault. He tumbled back down. The only damage done by his scatter gun was a hole in the response boat, well above the waterline.

I examined Rene Terazzo . . . correction . . . a hole in the response boat and an enormous, gaping hole in Terazzo's chest. I pushed him over the side.

Hector disappeared down the galley steps, dragged the body back up and dropped it near the rail.

"This is the piece of shit that terrorized our town for a month or so, and probably all of the

Keys for much longer. Anyone wish to offer a prayer? . . . Anybody? . . . No? . . . okay." Without ceremony he tossed the body over the side.

Henry had been listening and nodding his approval to all that had gone on. "Any ideas for those on the jet boat?' he asked over the bullhorn.

I thought for a moment. "I have a couple," I said. "We could sink their boat, we could take them back to jail but that could get messy, or we could give them each a few bucks and set them free right where we sit.

You hear stories all the time of an immigrant who comes to America with only $50 and through hard work becomes successful. I have enough cash in my pocket to give each one a hundred bucks."

"Except," Henry said, "They are not allowed to return to the U.S."

"How about the yacht and zodiac?" Hector asked.

"The law of the sea," Paul joined in, "You find it abandoned, it's yours!

Henry walked to the edge, looked down at the jet boat and asked, "How many of you are U.S. citizens?"

Bunny asked the others in Spanish as she raised her hand. "Just me," she replied. "There is a box in a drawer below with all the passports."

Paul knew where they were. He retrieved them for Henry, who thumbed through them all, then tossed the appropriate passport to its owner.

"Bunny goes back with us," he announced. "Garrett, bring that jet boat key. Hector, fill their gas tank from the yacht. Paul, help Bunny into the Coast Guard vessel. Gil," he yelled to the guardsman on the gun, "put the woman in the brig."

I smiled at Henry's efficiency as I walked over to the jet boat, dropped a key into the old man's hand, then a hundred dollar bill to each of them. They didn't deserve it, but it may be the difference between starving and staying alive until they reach home.

Paul ran to the galley at my request and brought water, canned goods and an opener and dropped them into the jet boat. Gas refilled, the small boat with three aboard headed southwest toward Hispaniola.

It was about 4:40 p.m. The sea was still calm, the weather still quite warm . . . nothing had changed, except Paul was finally safe. And Gary Thune was no more.

50

Friday, Oct 18
6:55 p.m.
Visit with Fox

We were returning to Key West--Paul, Hector and I in the yacht; Henry, his guardsman and Bunny Thune on the response boat. I left a message for Paul's father who was not in his office. Then I called Liz. She was ecstatic.

"Hurry home, Bossman. I wish I had been with you; I *should* have been with you. But you are bringing Paul home. Yippie! Paul is safe!"

"And how are you doing, my Love?"

"Woohooo! I'm your love, Bossman! Oh, I love you! And now I'm doing great!"

"It was a generic 'my love', Fox. Don't get all that gooey and slobbery on me."

"Ah, com'on, Gumshoe. You know you love me."

"Okay, I love you. Now, how about them 49ers?"

"Cute."

"Seriously, what does Nell say about you?"

"I've been shot."

"Cute."

"Nell says I was shot four times, I have eight holes in me. The physical therapist says my leg and hand, with hard work, will be as good as new within a week, three weeks for my shoulder and I can have a steak as soon as you take me out of here . . . so long as you stab it and hold it still while I cut it.

Oh! Nell says if we go for a romantic canoe ride in the moonlight, you'll have to paddle."

"So, your tummy's fine? No damage to the vitals?"

"No. I can even drink water with no leaks. Bullet went through left love handle. Hurts like crazy, but it hit nothing major."

"We'll be there in a little over two hours. I'll see you as soon as we land."

I called Pop; he was saddened to hear Liz was involved in a shooting, but delighted with the success of the operation.

"When will you be home, Son?" he asked. "Amy has volunteered to answer the phones at your agency, but she can't tell potential clients anything definitive."

"Oh, Pop! I didn't expect anyone to do that. Just leave my message on the answering machine, you know--'on assignment'."

"Amy wanted to do something special, Alan. You saved her life--that's something a person doesn't forget. By the way, her attorney fast-tracked the transfer papers for the Fallbrook home from Sharon Etts to her--with Peter Gunn assisting." (I covered this adventure in a previous writing.)

We chatted for a few minutes more; the special assignment I had given to Pop was finished. He was looking for something more to do.

"Go on a cruise with Rita, Pop. Travel the world. Write about your firefighting escapades. You don't need me to provide a platform to keep you occupied."

"I know, Son. Speaking of Rita, we are becoming rather serious. You may find yourself batching by next summer."

"WooHoo, Pop! I'll buy rice and a suit!"

"Wait a minute, Alan. You have us going all the way . . . uh, so to speak. We're talking about moving in together. That will give you some privacy . . . and an upstairs room for a nursery."

"Now who's being funny?" I laughed. "Looking to be a grandpa? Hey, maybe I'll have a kid brother instead." We both had a good laugh as we hung up.

The General called almost immediately.

"Garrett, you have my son! Good man! Where is he now?"

"He's sitting beside me at the controls of a small yacht. We're returning to Key West from about a hundred miles at sea. Here he is," I said, turning the phone over to Paul.

"Hi, Dad. Thanks for sending Mr. Garrett after me. . . . I'm sorry, I really blew it. . . . Yes. . . . Yes . . . I won't. . . . I promise . . . I love you, too. . . . Mr. Garrett says he'll send me home tomorrow . . ." Paul handed my phone back.

"I'll put him up in a motel for tonight and return him tomorrow morning on a plane, Sir," I explained. "Send me an e-mail with orders, I'll take him to Miami and send him wherever you wish. Good evening, Sir. . . . You're very welcome, General."

* * *

Half an hour later, we pulled into the marina. Francisco Bardos was waiting at the end of the pier. He guided the yacht into it's original slip, then he untied the zodiac and maneuvered it into it's slip while Paul and I walked to the end of the main walkway.

Francisco joined us. "Jennifer tells me she has a room on hold for you and the young fellow in case you need it. I'll drive you to . . ."

"No need, Francisco, but thanks. I have a car. I need to go to the hospital. I promised Liz I'd be there as soon as we pulled in. I'll call your boss and the Chief . . . see if they want to get together at *The Hungry Pelican* for pie and coffee; you're welcome to join us."

"Thanks, No. I'm on my way home; I'm already late for dinner."

We parted. I was tired. I was giving Paul the litany of things I had yet to do when my phone rang. It was Hector.

"Garrett, Francisco said something about us meeting for pie and coffee, but Henry and I are going to bow out. It's been a tough day."

I barely hung up when the phone rang . . . Rachel.

"Oh! Hi, Rachel. I . . ."

"Stop, Alan! Let me talk, please!"

"Ooops, sorry. Say on, Rachel."

"We had some good days, nights and in-betweens, didn't we? I've been to your office twice, asking about you. The girl there, Amy, is waiting anxiously for your return. Your lady friend, that artist who made your sign, was there during one visit worrying about your safe return. Meanwhile, you're sailing around south Florida with that bitch of a partner of yours, that one you call Fox!

Keep my Cadillac, your entourage, your little flock, Alan! Whatever we had is officially over!"

She hung up before I could say anything. I simply looked at the phone and shook my head.

Paul heard no part of the conversation, but he understood by its one-sidedness that it was a lecture not dissimilar from the one he would be expecting, once back home.

"Is everything alright, Mr. Garrett?"

"Everything is just fine, son, and getting better every minute."

I continued with my list, more to myself than to Paul.

"I probably owe a bundle on the repairs to the motel room. I'll stop there and settle our account. But, first things first."

I headed for the hospital, taking Paul with me.

Up to the fourth floor. Jackie pointed to Room 411. "Leave her here tonight. Take her home tomorrow, early afternoon."

We walked in. Fox was sitting up. When she saw our smiling faces, she lit up.

"Oh, Gumshoe!" she squealed with delight, "I'm so glad you're home and safe."

I leaned down, gave her a long kiss. "I'm safe, Liz, and it's over. Gary Thune is shark bait, Bunny Thune is in Hector's cell, others in his hit squad are no more, and others will never come back into U.S. waters. Our job here is done, Liz."

I invited Paul to come forward. "This young man is Paul Maggorie." I introduced Paul to Liz.

"Ma'am. I understand you risked your life to save me. I don't know how I can thank you enough."

"Just be a good kid, a better man, and always try to do the honorable thing," she said. "That's thanks enough."

Liz asked tons of questions; I answered them all . . . then it was my turn.

"How did Martaise manage to access our motel room, Fox? Haven't I taught you better?"

"I actually invited her, in a manner of speaking. I saw a female with a camera; she looked a lot like Miss Martaise, so I decided to . . ."

"You left the motel room unlocked?"

"I left the motel room unlocked. You're fast, Gumshoe. I think our partnership should be permanent."

"Dumbest think I've ever heard of, Fox."

"But, my brain was lightening fast, Gumshoe. I kept my hand on my Beretta at all times, even when I went into the girl's room to tinkle."

"She's an assassin, Fox! For crying out loud! Your lightening fast brain could have wasted your slower-than-molasses butt!" I was furious.

"Stop the act, Bossman. You would have done the same. Admit it!"

"That's different!"

"See? You men!" she said in mock disgust, "think you have all the macho rights God ever handed out. I thought you'd be proud of me."

"I am proud of you, Fox, I just . . ."

"And I'm pretty sure she's no longer an assassin."

"Continue," I said. "Then what happened?"

"As I started out the bathroom door she shot, I think, about four shots. She hit my finger and my left shoulder as I was coming out. She was standing almost in front of me.

I shot her point blank, twice in the neck or upper chest area; she dove behind a bed and fired a few more times, hit my leg and my stomach . . . funny . . . every bullet felt like a bee sting.

When she raised up a bit I shot three or more times; I know I hit her in the forehead. That's all I remember, but I knew she was dead. There was a lot of blood. Next thing I remember was waking up in the hospital. Now I'm tired, Bossman. I think the nurse must have given me a magic pill."

I gave her another kiss. "I'm taking Paul to Miami tomorrow morning, be back around noon. We're going home tomorrow, Liz. Get some sleep."

"Nice meeting you, Paul. Have a good life."

We said goodnight to Jackie.

Paul and I dropped by the restaurant to have pie a'la mode and coffee. The place was thinning out–almost closing time.

"Is she your wife, Mr. Garrett?"

"No. An investigator in my agency."

"Why does she call you Gumshoe?"

"Long story, but short version? a slang term for a private eye."

"Oh. Sometimes you call her Liz, sometimes Fox . . . why?"

I handed him my card. "No more questions."

51

Friday, Oct 18
7:35 p.m.
Just Another Day

John simply shrugged when we walked into the motel office. "Sorry, no room available . . . for you, Mr. Garrett; Boss's orders."

I looked over the bill he presented for the room damage, and opened my wallet. Twenty-one hundred dollars. *Less than I thought.*

"What about lost revenue?" I asked. "You're probably looking at three days to make the repairs. Let's call it twenty-five hundred even."

He smiled. I handed him my credit card and asked for my suitcases.

We headed to *The Chelsea House*. Dave was expecting us.

"Only one night, I think, Dave. Is Jennifer home? If she is, have her come to our room in a half hour, please."

Paul was taking a shower when the phone rang. It was Inspector Morris from Manhattan Beach.

"Inspector! This is a nice surprise! What's up?"

"Garrett, when are you going to get your ass off that giant lizard-infested swampland and bring it home?"

"You miss me, huh?"

"I spoke with your dad an hour ago. He says you're coming home tomorrow. Something about Liz getting shot. Is she okay?"

"A few flesh wounds, but we're packing up tomorrow and heading back. That's why you called, Morris? To check on Liz? I appreciate that."

"No, there's more, Garrett. We have a few problems . . . I could use some private talent."

"Like what, Morris?"

"Big increase in bad drugs on our streets for one, and uh, . . ."

"Bullshit, Morris. You just want a place to hang out and some decent booze at the end of the day."

"Well, there is that . . . but no! I'm serious, Alan. Shorthanded as always, as you know. Manhattan Beach isn't what it was when you were a kid.

The other problem has to do with the people I work with."

Paul emerged from the bathroom with a towel wrapped around his waist.

I cupped my hand over the phone mouthpiece. "Grab that bed," I told Paul. "I'll use this one." Paul tucked himself into the bed. I tossed him a book to read.

Paul caught it mid-air. "Hmmm. *A Ranger's Tale—the Jacks' Vendetta* . . . is this any good?"

"Yes. I picked it up at the airport in Los Angeles; finished it before I landed. Easy read."

Then going back to the phone, "Sorry, Morris," I said, "but if you have such a problem, wouldn't it be for an in-house Internal Affairs to solve?"

"Should be, but I'd rather explain in person, over a cognac."

"I'm sure you would," I laughed.

There was a knock on the door.

"Hang on," I said to Morris.

"No," he said with a laugh. "Sounds like Grand Central Station there; call me when you're settled at home."

I opened the door to Jennifer. "You wanted to see me, Sir?"

"Hi, Jennifer come in, please. Jennifer, this is Paul . . . Paul, no need to stand, this is the Key West Harbor Master, Jennifer Little." They said 'Hi' to each other.

"I asked you here for two reasons, Jen. First, we're going home tomorrow, so I wanted to say goodbye . . ."

"Oh, we will miss you and Fox, Mr. Garrett." She came over and hugged my neck.

"And," I continued, "I would like permission to set up a trust account for you. One that you can tap into with no penalty for early withdrawal, but one that will mature in, let's say 2025. You should have such an instrument in a Key West Bank; if not, I'll have Liz sleuth one out for you."

"You don't need to do that, Mr. Garrett. I'm doing just fine."

"True, I don't. But, I want to encourage you to continue your education without worrying over your next step, financially."

"What can I say?" She hugged me again.

Paul piped up, "Just say thanks, Jennifer."

She opened the door, "Yes, of course. Thank you, Mr. Garrett. I'll never forget you."

"Same here," I said as she stepped out into the early evening and closed the door.

I was just preparing to shower when my phone rang again. It was the General.

"Garrett, I've made arrangements with the Coast Guard. They'll fly that derelict son of mine out of the Boca Chica Air Base tomorrow morning at 8:45, so there's no need to drive all the way up to Miami."

"Boca Chica? The military base? You must have some clout, General."

"Just enough to get my boy on a flight to D.C. The V.P. signed off on it. The flight was a dead head--two decorated seamen also on the flight."

"That's excellent, Sir. Saves me a long drive."

"I figured you had things to do in California, so I made a few phone calls. Your Commander Waite tells me you shook things up in his town. Sometimes a fresh set of eyes picks up what others have become indifferent to, Son."

"Oh, it wasn't all me, Sir. It started with my associate being discovered by the kidnappers while trying to keep track of Paul. Kidnappers happened to have ties to international crime."

"Still, they tell me you did some good work while there . . . you and your sidekick."

"Nothing more than others would do, Sir."

"Oh! By the way, I'll settle up with you the same way as the retainer if that works for you, Garrett."

"Sir, your retainer was $70K; I think that should cover everything."

"Right. Well, have Paul on that 8:45 flight tomorrow morning if you would, Garrett."

"Ha! Your derelict son, as you say, will be there, Sir."

52

Saturday, Oct 19
6:05 a.m.
Goodbye to the Derelict Son
Goodbye Florida

Paul and I had breakfast at *The Hungry Pelican.* Sam, Ernie and all of our old-timer friends were assembled to say their goodbyes. I introduced Paul to them.

"So you're the young feller that caused all the ruckus around here, huh?" Ernie asked him, laughing.

"I guess so," Paul said.

"Most fun we've had in years, wasn't it, Sam?"

"The whole town," Sam shot back. "Not this much excitement since Blackbeard, right fellas?" Affirmation, accompanied by peals of laughter rose from around the dining room.

We finished our meal, waved goodbye and headed for the Boca Chica Airbase. We were stopped at the gate.

"Sorry, Sir, no civilians allowed."

"Please call a Major Bechtel--travel officer. He's expecting us."

He made the call. Five minutes later a dark blue utility van pulled up at the gate. An officer with a clip board stepped out, poked his head in my driver's side of our vehicle.

"Paul Maggorie?"

"That's me," Paul smiled.

"Come with me, Son."

I gave Paul a hug, shook his hand and bid him farewell.

"Thank you for everything, Mr. Garrett," he said. "I'll miss you and Miss Fox."

The officer from the van bent down to take a closer look at me. "Garrett? AFOSI Alan Garrett?" he asked.

"That's me," I confessed, mimicking Paul.

"An honor to meet you, Sir." He saluted.

I laughed, "No need, Just plain Alan Garrett, P.I., Manhattan Beach, California."

I watched until the van disappeared inside a hangar, then I made my way back to Key West.

* * *

It would have been nice to have said goodbye to Hector or Henry, but neither answered when I called. But, after all, I thought—it's Saturday. They're probably enjoying their families.

I spent the next couple of hours walking along the marina, stopping at Ginny's kiosk to feed birds and chatting with a few fishermen and women returning with catches from a morning on the water.

At 11:50 a.m. my phone rang. It was Nurse Jackie. "Mr. Garrett! Liz is ready to go home."

"Be right there."

Driving to the hospital, my phone rang again. "Garrett, Hector here. You're planning on going home today, right? Do you mind swinging by before you leave? I'd like your written statement. That FBI lady says she needs corroboration of a couple of things. Won't take a minute. She's here now."

"Sorry," I said, "I'm headed for the hospital before anything else."

"Just a minute," he said. I heard muffled voices, then he came back with, "Continue to the hospital, pick up Fox and bring her. FBI says she'll wait."

Liz was waiting in the lobby in a wheelchair. I was surprised to see Marge sitting beside her.

"Good morning, Mr. Garrett," Marge said. "I found Liz sitting down here all by herself, waiting. She hasn't even had lunch yet."

"You're kidding!" I turned to Liz, "They didn't feed you? Oh, Man! Let's go to *The Hungry Pelican*, Liz. I'll buy that steak you wanted."

"I am a bit hungry, Bossman. Don't know if I can eat a steak and baked potato, but it sure sounds good after the hospital grub."

We walked out without looking back at Jackie. Marge said goodbye and walked across the street to her home. I assisted Fox into the rental car and we headed to *The Hungry Pelican*.

"Damn! I forgot, I told Hector I would stop for a couple of minutes to give a short deposition. Do you mind, Fox?"

"No, of course not, Gumshoe. We can say our goodbyes to Hector and whatever cops are there."

"Yeah, well the FBI is supposed to be there as well."

"Oh! The Brain!"

"Yeah."

We walked in and were immediately ushered into the conference room. Around the table sat almost everyone we had become friends with in Key West.

There was Teresa Hughes--the FBI agent, Hector, Ernie, Sam, Jennifer, Marge, Jackie, Nell, and Tim White. Only Henry was missing. We were seated. Hector made sure I was sitting beside Teresa. Next to me on the other side was Jennifer, then came Fox. I frowned. One chair was empty; *why seat her beside me?*

Hector stood. "Ladies and Gentlemen," he started, "There's wine on the table, please fill your glasses." We all complied. "Now a toast!" he continued. "Today we're saying goodbye to two people we hope will never come back to Key West."

"Here, here!" came shouts and laughter from around the table.

"But if they ever *do* come back down here," Teresa added, "make sure you lose my phone number." Laughter and boos met her, but she wasn't finished. "I want only to come as far south as *The St. Regis Bal Harbour Resort* in Miami." More laughter and boos. "Oh, c'mon, I'm kidding!"

At that moment, Henry walked through the rear door pushing a cart. Marge jumped up to assist him. They set, in front of Fox and me, large plates of Blackened Cubera Snapper on a bed of steamed brown and wild rice, mixed with snow peas, garlic cloves and roasted tomato halves.

Marge continued around the table until twelve plates were served. Then Henry stood behind the last place at the table.

"Another toast," he smiled. "Everyone lift a fork. It's been my pleasure to prepare this meal, but you should know, this is wild caught Cubera Snapper, caught by Miss Fox, here--our own favorite Californian."

"Here, here!" shouted Hector. Once again, all joined in.

After one bite, Ernie raised his glass. "If they decide to come back, they git thirty minutes free on my boat before I start the clock at 100 bucks an hour." More laughter. Of course, we toasted the chef and the server as well as our host.

At 2:30 p.m. Fox and I said our goodbyes to the fair city, first to the Key West International Airport, from there to Miami, then the journey to LAX, and from there a short taxi home to Manhattan Beach. We took turns saying it to each other; the sound of it, *home to Manhattan Beach . . .* like nectar to our minds.

We dropped off Fox's rental and hopped aboard a shuttle to Key West International.

Epilogue

Wednesday, December 11, 2019
11:20 p.m.
Manhattan Beach

The dusty flip board in my study at home had been sitting empty since before I left for Florida. It was identical to the one at my office. One side was cork for any correspondence, photos, and articles between interested parties in a matter; the other side white for any notes I might consider jotting down.

When we walked into our office back in October we discovered that board still had pictures Fox had sent from Florida . . . those silly, damn kids that were with Paul, and later found dead inside that old derelict trawler, *The Blue Moon.*

I felt like I'd been gone for months rather than just days. I watched Fox clear that one off and tuck all our notes in a file box and set it in the empty office. That was the day she discovered her leg pain.

Now, sitting in my study, I sighed, took a sip of Martell and pondered the new project I had agreed Fox and I would accept.

I studied the dusty cork board for a moment . . . opened a new bottle and poured two fingers of Martell. I took a swig, then reached for a photo of Bradley Swazer and pinned it to the board. Morris had given me a few more photos and a couple of depositions yet to tack to the board. Before I start filling it with photos and notes, I thought, *I'd better get a damp sponge and dust it.*

Pop came through the door from a date with Rita.

"Son, are you going to be okay here alone?" I poured him a short Martell, smiled, and began wiping down the board. Pop followed my every motion, asking questions--first, Rachel, then Amy and finally Liz. It was going to be a long night.

* * *

Much has happened since our return to California. A few examples and thoughts . . .

Fox is walking now without a wince or *'yip'* of pain. We thought her leg wound was healing nicely, but she developed an infection somewhere along the line; fortunately she discovered the telltale signs . . . the redness, the swelling. She ended up back in the hospital for two nights while the medicine men and women worked their magic.

* * *

General Maggorie, God bless him, direct-deposited $180,000 into Fox's credit card account. I called him to complain.

"Garrett!" he nearly broke my eardrum, "those monsters demanded a million dollars for the return of Paul! You hear me? One million dollars! I figure a quarter of that is a bargain."

I wasn't about to argue. I sighed, "Thank you, Sir. Glad to be of service."

* * *

Pop wasn't kidding. He's planning to move in with Rita, share expenses, do the live-together thing. He presently hangs his hat upstairs in the bungalow he signed over to me years ago.

Now, Rita is just down the cul-de-sac, only four or five houses away. I can see it as a win-win for Pop. I can also see it as a win-not-so-much for me: I'll have two coffees to serve most mornings, I'll have a woman in my kitchen when I rise and throw on my knickers just to make coffee.

But I applaud Pop. I suppose it will all be worked out . . . to Pop's satisfaction. And I congratulate Rita. She is getting a good man . . . my Pop. Their target date is January one. Oh, they'll be moving to Rita's, but this is still Pop's Place. I won't take his key away from him.

* * *

The world is not the same. I've never been one to jump into the political milieu, and I stand by that. But--but, we have some serious political problems within our U.S. borders.

Back in September as I was preparing my trip to Florida, I smelled a political fight coming in our U.S. Congress, but I didn't know to what extent it would lower our stature on the world stage. I fear it will.

* * *

On another front, it does look like Morris'

precinct needs a bit of outside help. He explained it this way . . . between two short glasses of Martell . . .

"Our budget for police work is stretched to the limit, Garrett. It doesn't allow us to have a full time Internal Affairs officer, and we're completely backed up with day to day work. At this moment I'm trying to find time to investigate an officer-involved shooting.

Cop says perp brandished a gun in a pharmacy robbery; he says it was a good shoot; pharmacist and two patrons agree. They say perp had a gun, but three others say no gun--one of them adamant. No gun was found." I raised my eyebrows, added a bit to Morris' glass. He smiled and continued.

"Then two weeks ago, we had a breach in lock-up. Three guns, paperwork on three separate cases, all missing. For how long? We don't know. All at one time? We don't know. We need some help. I can pay on a per diem basis for a private investigator. Are you interested?"

"Can't Swazer investigate your shooter case? He's competent, aggressive, probably needs the money . . ."

"I can't, Garrett. Bradley is the shooter."

* * *

Liz and I discussed it. We decided to help Morris and Swazer out. And so . . . . I tacked Bradley Swazer to my cork board.

www.ingramcontent.com/pod-product-compliance
Lightning Source LLC
Chambersburg PA
CBHW060951120726
47910CB00002B/582